COWBOY DOMINATION

Stacey Espino

MENAGE AMOUR

Siren Publishing, Inc.
www.SirenPublishing.com

A SIREN PUBLISHING BOOK
IMPRINT: Ménage Amour

COWBOY DOMINATION
Copyright © 2011 by Stacey Espino

ISBN-10: 1-61034-268-2
ISBN-13: 978-1-61034-268-1

First Printing: January 2011

Cover design by Jinger Heaston
All cover art and logo copyright © 2011 by Siren Publishing, Inc.

PUBLISHER
Siren Publishing, Inc.
www.SirenPublishing.com

DEDICATION

To the night time muse that keeps me awake with naughty ideas for my next release.

COWBOY DOMINATION

STACEY ESPINO
Copyright © 2011

Chapter One

Callie ripped the letter into four, then eight pieces before hurling the white bits through the air like oversized confetti. She reared out of the wooden chair and paced the country kitchen with a seething anger. Another eviction notice. Her grandparents' house had been paid off decades ago, but the state kept raising their property taxes to the point they couldn't afford to pay them. It just wasn't right that wealthy landowners could drive small farmers off their land with a phone call to the nearest crooked politician.

When she noticed her grandpa standing in the doorway, her anger melted away like the butter on her morning toast.

"Don't tell me that was a love letter from Josh," he said with concern etched on his aged face.

"It was nothing, Grandpa. You shouldn't be up. Do you need something?"

"You'll have me bed-bound in no time. I'm still quite capable, child."

She smiled gently. "I know you are. I just want you to take it easy. Doctor's orders, remember?"

"I may be up in years, but I can still handle a rifle. Is that Josh boy causing you heartache?"

Her grandfather, such an old-school cowboy, and she loved him more than life itself. Even in his late seventies, he had his wits and kept in good shape. Not even after her grandmother's death, some four years earlier, did his health falter. Not the way it had since those bastards tried to take his land. Callie vowed not to allow him to know what was currently waging with the attempted takeover of their farm. As far as he was concerned, all was well, and his only mission was to get well. She'd find one way or another to pay those taxes and get the law off their backs.

"You know Josh would never hurt me. In fact, he'll be over this afternoon with a shipment of feed."

"Good to hear. Now be a doll and fetch your grandpa his pipe. I'll be on the porch."

Callie forgot about the shredded letter and made her way to her grandpa's small bedroom and located his pipe and tobacco on his night side table. Her earliest memories were of him rocking back and forth in the old wooden rocker on the front porch with a pipe between his lips. As she padded her way through the bungalow, she heard the slam of a truck door. It was too early for Josh to show up. He had fields to clear first thing in the morning.

Pushing open the whiny screen door, she noted the tall, thin man sauntering up to the front porch with a briefcase in hand. Trouble had shown up at the front door. Her mind whirled as she thought of ways to deal with the stranger while avoiding upsetting her grandpa. She had no doubt the visit had something to do with the frequent phone calls and letters threatening to take their farm.

"Good mornin' to you," said her grandpa.

"Mr. Johnson, I'd like to have a word with you, if you don't mind."

Callie bounded off the porch, placing herself between the two men. "Can I help you?" She narrowed her eyes at the man, willing him away with her most heated death stare.

"My name's Jack Smith. I've been sent by the Black Corporation about some important business matters."

"If you need to talk business, you can talk with me."

The man hesitated for a moment, appearing as though he'd like to argue, but held back. His thin, mousy brown hair fluttered as a warm, light breeze swept by. He stood out like a sore thumb in his navy blue business suit, surrounded by pasture. Callie felt like a child next to him in her white cotton summer dress. But she wasn't a child, and if these land thieves thought they could show up and bring her grandpa grief, they had another thing coming.

"And who might you be, young lady?"

Callie ground her molars together at his patronizing tone. He might be old enough to be her daddy, but he sure as hell wasn't. She had no daddy—no mother, either. It was just Callie and her grandpa, and she couldn't lose him, too.

"I'm Callie Johnson."

"Ah, I see. So you must be the one giving me the runaround." He shook his too-thin face and cast his beady eyes on her with disapproval. "Dangerous game you're playing here. You can't play dumb and ignore the call of progress."

Her grandfather rose to his feet and braced himself on the porch railing with one hand.

"What's going on here? What's he talking about, Callie Lynn?" He only called her by both her names when he was angry. It was her only warning because he never raised his voice or hand toward her.

"Seems you have your head underwater in the flood of unpaid taxes for this property, Mr. Johnson. If you can't pay up, that's not a problem." He pulled out a folder from his open briefcase and held it up. "I've been authorized to pay a pretty penny for this home and the surrounding acreage."

Callie flipped her head back and forth between the men in attempts to gauge their expressions.

"Haven't you paid the taxes?" Her grandpa questioned her.

"Of course! This is all a big misunderstanding. Mr. Smith, perhaps we could discuss this at your office. My grandpa is a sick man and shouldn't be troubled with this nonsense."

"As you wish." He handed her a business card. "I'll expect to hear from you before the week is through, or I'll have no choice but to pay another visit." He whispered, for her ears only, "Next time, I'll be forced to bring the sheriff."

He nodded his head politely to her grandpa and turned back to his truck. She noted it was a company vehicle with a rearing black stallion as the logo for the Black Corporation. What a tangled web her life had become in such a short time. How in heaven's name was she expected to pay those back taxes? Even if she did come up with the money, they'd only find some other excuse to run them off the land.

Callie could adapt, but her grandpa was old and tired. He should spend all his last days in the only home he had ever known. Generations of Johnsons had worked this land, and memories of his beloved wife filled the picture-littered walls of the small bungalow. She had to do something.

"You sure you paid those taxes, Callie? It's not like a banker to come all the way out here for a house call."

"I'm sure, Grandpa. I'll go get the receipts in order and head over this afternoon and straighten it all out. Nothing to worry about."

She hated lying to him. It's not like she avoided her responsibilities. She worked the land harder than any man. From sunup until sundown, she maintained the farm all on her own. They only had a small herd now and a few planted fields. It should be enough to survive on. Had always been enough. Now, the bank wanted more than they were able to provide because they wanted their land, probably for oil, but she had no proof. Greedy vultures thrived off the poor and vulnerable.

Thank God she had Josh in her life. That was another story in itself. She loved him like the good friend he was, but he wanted more than she was willing to give. A farmer with no ambitions beyond the fields he plowed, no dreams, no hopes, was not the man for her. Josh was a sweetheart. Younger than she and raised good and proper by his parents, he'd make an excellent husband and provider. But she couldn't marry out of necessity or expectation. She may be a fool, but she still held on to hope for the elusive true love spoken about in fairy tales. If she never found it, the farm could keep her busy enough. But she wouldn't settle. Not even for Josh. If she were being perfectly honest, the boy was too downright sweet. He never had a harsh word for her, and no matter how cruelly she behaved, he took it. A real man wouldn't put up with half of her nonsense.

She found herself testing his limits when they were together. He deserved better than her, and she needed more than he could offer.

After slipping on some blue jeans and a clean T-shirt, she pulled her long blonde hair into a functional ponytail and then grabbed her truck keys to head out. She'd show up at the Black Corporation and give them a piece of her mind, all right. Surely someone there had a conscience. She was a reasonable woman. If she had to, she'd sell off most of the land to keep them happy. What really mattered was the home her grandpa occupied and the surrounding land.

Callie's truck skidded along the gravel drive as she plowed her way to the dirt road that would lead her to the Black Corporation.

Chapter Two

Colton Black interlocked his fingers behind his back as he studied the open fields through his office window. He loved a sun-kissed day and couldn't wait to head outside and get his hands dirty. At least six calves were close to birth, and he didn't want to miss the miracle sitting behind a desk. His skin crawled when he was confined behind four walls. He needed to be outdoors, working the land hands-on. But his new manager, Jack Smith, said it was important to make a daily appearance, being the head of the company. He'd never asked for the job, but, being the eldest, all responsibility had fallen onto his shoulders.

According to Jack, he should be stuffed in a suit and have his fingernails manicured, not spend his days rolling around in the hayfields like some common hick. He didn't blame Jack. He did his job well and just couldn't understand the appeal of the open land and old-fashioned hard work to a cowboy. Jack was a—what did they call them again—a metrosexual, or a so-called urban cowboy. Colton chuckled to himself as he turned back into the room.

Before he could bury himself in paperwork, Waylon burst through his office door like the place was on fire. "You've got to see this!" He turned and ran back the way he'd come without an explanation. With his curiosity peaked, Colton followed his brother's path through the main office to the parking area out front.

A small crowd had grown. Workers from the barns, employees from the office, and God knows who the others were. The focus of the melee was a petite little blonde firecracker cursing like a sailor. With her arms flailing, her plump breasts bounced under the cotton shirt she wore, no doubt braless by the looks of it. She directed her anger toward his other brother, Boyd, who looked more lost than a calf without its momma. He needed backup in a hurry.

"What's the trouble?" Colton asked after pushing his way through the small crowd.

"I'll tell you what the trouble is! This here big shot doesn't have a problem stealing a farm from an old man and a helpless woman. Whatever happened to honesty and integrity?"

"Whoa, there." He approached her as if dealing with a skittish, green-broke horse. If she referred to herself, she was no helpless woman by any means. Even the roughneck cowboys on his crew gave her a wide berth of space. "Why don't we go inside and talk about this?"

"And who might you be?"

"I'm Colton Black. This here is my brother, Boyd."

She crossed her arms over her chest, which plumped up her already full bosom. "Great. How many of you are there?"

"Three." Waylon stepped out of the crowd, pushing his mop of dirty-blond hair off his face. He looked way too pleased with himself. His youngest brother thought he was God's gift to women. Some of his whores would no doubt agree.

"Well, ain't this just dandy," she said before another curse. "Three grown men ganging up on a little old man. I hope you're all happy with yourselves."

"Please. Let's take this inside," he repeated with stronger authority. This time, he tapped her on the back in hopes she'd follow his direction. She jerked away from his touch as if he'd scalded her but continued on toward the office in an irritated march.

The bombshell had a tight ass with just the right amount of jiggle. A man could grab those full mounds and knead his fingers into the soft flesh. His cock stirred as he followed behind her. He turned only once to give the crowd a single look that sent them scattering back to their duties. Boyd and Waylon followed Colton. Whatever this girl was talking about concerned all of them. The Black Corporation was a family-run business. With their parents retired and enjoying the good life, it was up to the three brothers to keep things running smoothly. Where was Jack when you needed him? An irate citizen should blast her volatile energy on the manager, not the owners. God knows they paid him enough to deal with even worse situations.

"Have a seat," said Colton after the four of them had entered his office. Back into his claustrophobic prison when he had just gotten a taste of the sweet summer air.

"I'd rather stand." Of course she would. He assumed by now she'd rebut anything he said. A woman like her needed a solid spanking. He'd love to be the one to dish out that kind of punishment. Colton could already picture her sweet, plump ass reddened from his ministrations as she lay naked over his lap. His blood fired hot as his cock tightened in his pants. It had been awhile since he'd had a woman, and that denial was making itself known.

"Can you please explain what you're ranting about? What's your name? And what farm do you claim we're trying to steal?"

She took a deep breath, which appeared to take a herculean effort due to her heaving chest. "My name is Callie Johnson. I live with my grandpa, not twenty minutes from here. Ever since your company showed interest in our land, our taxes have climbed. Now, we're so behind, they're threatening to take our land."

"This is the first I've heard of this."

"Bullshit! I know all about you oil tycoons. You think you can buy everything, from land to people. But I'll tell you one thing for certain...I'm not for sale, and neither is my grandpa's land."

"Oil tycoons?" Colton chuckled. "Who told you that?"

Her irritated features softened for a moment then returned to their previous state. "What else could you be?"

"We're just cattle farmers, Ms. Johnson. We may have a big operation, but it's still the same hard work under the sun, just more of it."

"Cattle farmers? Then why do you need my land? Just to expand? I can rent you land. Hell, you can graze for free if you'd stop sicking your banker hound after us."

Waylon commented, with a tinge of disgust, "Jack." Colton's youngest brother never did like the manager they'd hired, but he didn't trust easily.

"Did Jack Smith pay you a visit?" Colton asked.

"He most certainly did. And don't forget the phone calls and letters. I don't like him one bit. He threatened to bring the sheriff to clear us off our land. Do you want my grandfather's bad health on your conscience? Or do you even have any morals?"

"Listen here, little lady. I'm trying to help you, but you're not making it very easy." Colton may have liked her fire, but she was balancing on a fine line by threatening his character. It was a challenge to fill his father's boots, one he took seriously. Who was he if he didn't measure up?

"If you want to help me, then tell the bank, the town council, whomever, that you have no interest in our land. Then maybe they'll lower our taxes to a manageable rate."

Colton really should have listened to his manager about being more knowledgeable on the business side of their operation. He preferred working hands-on with the cattle. If one of the brothers would know about any potential property purchase, it would be Boyd. He was the responsible one, the constant sensible voice around the ranch, reminding him of their father. "You know anything about this, Boyd?"

"As far as I know, Jack has plans to purchase a couple farms in the area. It's part of his redevelopment and growth plan. I really don't think we should decide anything without him here." Boyd's thumbs were hooked in the front loops of his Levi's. As he spoke with Callie, his eyes roamed up and down the length of her with a hunger similar to Colton's own. His two brothers had the same taste in women as he had—blonde, petite, curvy, with a lot of spunk. Made for some nasty fights growing up.

Right now, Colton needed his brother to diffuse the volatile situation because Jack hadn't been around all morning.

* * * *

Boyd didn't really have a clue what to do with the woman in front of him. When she had hopped out of her pickup truck in front of the office, she hadn't spared time in lashing him with a wicked tongue. He couldn't remember a thing she'd said, only a jumble of angry words that made him dizzy. How could he feel threatened by the little thing when he stood twice as broad and a good foot taller? It amused him, watching her. If anything, she gave the cowboys standing around the scene a nice show. She jumped around and swung her arms, all worked up, which only accentuated one fine feminine figure.

He'd had the urge to shut her up with a mind-numbing kiss, but by the looks of her, he'd likely get a kick in the groin for it.

Now that he was forced to listen to her complaint, he tried to recall exactly what Jack Smith had told him about the farm purchases. Just like Callie, Jack went on and on about business matters, but he only picked up the highlights. The new farms were an integral part of the Black Corporation's restructuring and growth plan. They'd already spent a small fortune researching the finer points, so scrapping the whole plan for the ramblings of one little woman seemed foolhardy. Even if she was the cutest thing he'd ever seen.

She had long blonde hair, pulled off her delicate face, the cutest little pixie nose, and bright blue eyes. She wore no makeup, but even without it, her lips were pink and pouty, begging to be nibbled. By him. Already, he noted his big brother eyeing her with lust. Seemed another competition was in the making. It was a game the three of them had played once too often. All three fought for the same woman time and time again, so they'd compete to see who could bed the target first. It may have sounded sleazy, but the Black brothers had their pick of women. Women who had no problem putting their shoes under their beds with no questions asked. It seemed good looks, a hard body, and a bank account with millions were a real turn-on to loose women.

The problem was that Boyd didn't want those kinds of women for keeps. Now that he was pushing thirty, his mind often drifted to family matters, settling down with the love of a good woman. Fine females were hard to come by. They were small, shiny gems in an ocean of buckle bunnies and gold diggers. Maybe he'd never find one.

Chapter Three

Callie hurried to prepare dinner. She usually cut her vegetables in the morning and left the meat to simmer in the Crock-Pot throughout the day. With her schedule out of whack because of her visit to the Black Corporation, she had to get dinner made and her mountain of chores done before it got too late.

As soon as she arrived home, she peeked in her grandpa's room and found him fast asleep. Watching his chest rise and fall in a gentle rhythm calmed the raging beast inside her. Those Black brothers were something else. Just bringing them to mind set a plethora of emotions alight within her. She hated them for what they represented but also desired them in an unholy way. All three of them were tall and built like quarterbacks. Broad shoulders, squared jaws, and dangerous blue eyes were just a few features that got her pulse racing.

As she'd stood under their scrutinizing glares, she had actually considered offering herself in exchange for her grandpa's land. She was that desperate, and God knows her kin was that important to her. Imagining dropping to her knees to please any one of those three cowboys didn't repulse her as it should. In fact, under other circumstances, she'd do it for free…with bells on.

Callie nicked her finger with the paring knife and cursed. A bead of blood welled up, and she brought it to her mouth. She shook her head, trying to force the lusty thoughts far, far away. The Blacks were still the enemy. She hated them! She'd left the office no better off than when she had arrived. Even as the owners of the company, they'd used some pitiful excuse that they had to consult their manager before making decisions. They didn't look like the type of men who took orders well or asked for permission for anything. It had to be an excuse to shut her up and move her along her way. If they thought she was some soft-spoken woman who cried at the drop of a hat, they knew nothing about her.

When the phone rang and she heard that familiar whiny voice that had haunted her for months, she knew her trip had been in vain.

"Ms. Johnson. I hear you've had a busy morning."

She bit her lower lip and forced herself to breathe deeply before responding. "So the Black brothers got you to call me? How convenient for them. Just hire some lackey to deal with all the unpleasantness of destroying lives."

"Now, now, Ms. Johnson. Be smart. The offer still stands, and in today's market, I'll assure you it's more than generous."

"Remind me to send out thank-you notes." The offer on the property may have been fair, more than fair, but sometimes, it wasn't about money. This was their family home, the place where all her grandpa's memories lived. She wouldn't sell for all the riches in the world.

"One way or another, we will have your property. It's only a matter of walking away peacefully or being forced out. I don't think your grandpa would care to be tossed out in the dead of night, now, do you?"

"Don't you dare mention him! And stop calling my house. I have nothing left to say to you. According to these papers, I have twelve more days to pay my back taxes."

"Good luck with that." The line went dead. Callie slammed the phone back on its cradle, lifted it, and slammed it again. Shit! She'd forgotten about her grandpa asleep in the next room. Her mind was ready to explode with so many worries. Callie massaged her temples and took deep breaths to calm herself and fight off the headache threatening to overtake.

A soft rap on the front door forced her heart back into a frantic rhythm. No, she'd just hung up the phone with Jack Smith, so it couldn't be him. She had twelve days, so the sheriff or bank couldn't come and throw her to the curb just yet.

On the other side of the screen door stood a welcome sight. Josh Evans. The only person, besides her grandpa, who seemed to give two shits about her. After the day she'd had, she craved his familiar scent and warm smile, dimples and all.

"Josh, what time is it?"

"I came by earlier but saw the truck gone, so I thought I'd come back later. You don't mind, do you?"

"No, of course not." The screen smacked shut after she joined Josh on the front porch. She wrapped her arms up around his neck and rested her head on his shoulder. He may not have been tall and built like the Blacks, but he was a good man. He would never hurt her. Callie'd had all the evil she could deal with for one day. It would be nice to let it all go and let someone take care of her for a while, but that was a luxury not afforded to her. She had to be strong, in control.

Josh's body went stiff, and then he slowly draped her lower back with his arms. "What's the matter, Callie?"

She couldn't deny her mood because she wasn't a hugger. In fact, Josh was so used to her cold shoulder it surprised her he stuck around. Callie had too wild a spirit to settle down with a man like Josh Evans. Any other woman would give her right leg for a husband like him, but she only imagined herself trapped in a kitchen, kids grabbing at her legs, bored to tears. Nope. Not for her.

"Nothin'. Just having some trouble paying the bills."

"Why didn't you tell me?"

She pulled out of his loose embrace. "It's nothing new, and it's not your concern, Josh. I'm handling everything just fine."

"I'm here for you, Callie. Anything you need, you just have to ask. You know that, don't you?" His sincerity, the love in his boyish blue eyes, melted her heart. He did more than enough around the place to help her. Living only two farms over, he offered to harvest her hayfields, help with the small herd of cattle, and tend to any repairs around the place. Though she did most of the work herself, she appreciated the helping hand.

As if on cue, to prove her wrong for refusing his help, a truck and horse trailer traveled down the gravel path toward the house. Now what?

They both turned to watch as a portly man in a red and black plaid shirt and tan cowboy hat stepped out of the truck. As he approached the porch, another man began opening the trailer. Chains clattered and metal boomed when the ramp dropped to the ground.

"Can I help you?"

He held out a stapled pack of papers. "I'm under authority to take two Quarter Horse geldings into my possession."

"What!" She snatched the papers from the man and did a visual sweep of the legal document. Repo men? "You can't take my horses!"

"Them there papers say we can."

"But I have twelve days to pay the taxes." She hopped off the porch in an attempt to see what the other man was doing. The late afternoon sun blinded her. She held the papers over her eyes to get a better look. He approached the barn with a limp in his right leg.

"This ain't about taxes. Apparently, you have an unpaid bill at the local feed store. They have a legal right to take your possessions until you pay up."

"Mr. McGraw would never do this! We've had an account with him for decades." She felt frantic, her mind spinning around a mile a minute. Of the two horses, one was her pride and joy—Paddy. God, she loved that horse. He was eight years old, given to her on her sixteenth birthday by her grandpa. He'd been just two years then, and she'd named him Paddy after her childhood obsession with Paddington Bear. They were the same color and had the same intelligent eyes.

"Look. Read the papers, lady. I'm just doing my job." He spun on his heel to return to his truck. Callie followed behind him close enough to smell the jerky on his breath. When she saw the other man gone and the barn doors wide open, she ran ahead, her heart beating frantically.

"You're not taking him!" She tugged Paddy's halter as the stranger led her horse out of his stall. "He's mine."

"Sorry, but if you make trouble, we'll have to get the sheriff involved." Callie ducked under the horse's neck and physically tried to remove the man's hand. Paddy wasn't a car or big screen television they could just come and repossess. He was part of the family, her heart. She knew damn well they wouldn't take proper care of him. In fact, they'd more than likely abuse the animal. Paddy had a feisty spirit, not unlike her own, and he didn't fancy strangers.

When she started pounding on the man's chest, a set of arms snaked around her and shackled her wrists with strong hands before pulling her back. She tilted her head to the side. "Josh? What are you doing?" Her shock morphed into anger. "Let me go!"

"Callie, do you want to end up in jail? Just let them do their job, and then we'll deal with it afterwards."

"No!" She stomped like a stubborn child. The legal route hadn't aided her to date. When she paid her taxes and followed the book, the state royally screwed her because some spoiled, rich brothers wanted her land. She wanted to scream from the injustice. For once she wished Josh would scrap the good boy act and stand up for her.

Without any other choice, she watched the two hired men load the two horses into the oversized trailer. The sound of metal contacting metal when they closed the tailgate traveled all the way up her spine. She wanted to cry, but wouldn't. She wanted to be comforted, but wouldn't find what she needed. The driver dipped his hat and boarded the truck. Gravel scattered as they made a wide arch to exit the property. They'd take everything from her if she let them. Hadn't her life been enough of a struggle? How much strength was she expected to possess?

Chapter Four

Josh accompanied Callie to the Black Corporation. He slouched in the passenger seat, cleaning his nails with his keys. Disgusting. Things she normally let slide irritated her. Josh wasn't on good ground with her after allowing Paddy to be confiscated without a single protest.

After her horses were taken from her, she'd made a few phone calls. It was those bastard Black brothers who had pressured Mr. McGraw into signing the repossession orders. They wanted to make her life as miserable as possible in hopes that she'd cave and sell the farm to them. If they thought she was furious during her last visit, she had a surprise for them. Unfortunately, Josh insisted on coming along to be the voice of reason.

At this point, she didn't even care if they threw her into jail. She planned on giving them a piece of her mind. By the way they devoured her with their eyes the last time she visited, they probably thought she was some blonde bimbo, good for only one thing. They had a lot to learn. Callie was a survivor. When her own mother had abandoned her to her grandparents after she was born, she learned to develop a thick skin as a child. It wasn't easy knowing she had no daddy and her mother wanted nothing to do with her, especially living in the Bible Belt. Amazing how cruel people could be. When her grandma died, she'd had to take over too many responsibilities to count. She was glad to do it for the sake of her grandpa, especially after he grew sick, but the weight of the world was on her shoulders. Bottling up emotions made her a hostile woman. She really didn't like herself. Callie could envision a life where she had no worries. She'd ride the open fields on Paddy, the wind whipping back her hair, a smile on her face. If only.

Back in the familiar parking lot of the Black Corporation, Callie bounded ahead of Josh, hoping to cause some trouble before he could stop her. She pushed open the glass doors to the reception area, finding only the secretary at her desk.

"I'm looking for Colton Black. Any one of the Blacks, for that matter."

"I'm sorry, there's no one in the office. One of them should be out back in the barn. They're prepping for a branding."

Callie focused on not letting out her steam on the innocent secretary. She appeared to be in her early fifties, with shoulder-length brown hair and dark eyes. They should be blue. Something about middle-aged women brought out all her vulnerabilities. They made her recoil into herself, as if they could possibly cause more damage to her psyche than her own mother had managed. The little girl inside her wanted to impress, to beg for acceptance, even though these women were only reflections of the woman she never knew.

"Thank you."

Callie retreated from the office that suddenly felt smaller than a henhouse closing in on her. Bursting back into the fresh open air, she collided with Josh, who reached out and steadied her. "Find who you're looking for?"

"The barn." She didn't wait to explain, but followed the beaten path, crossed several gates, and entered the open end of the main barn. There were cowboys just about everywhere, doing one thing or another, but they didn't concern her. She was focused, her eyes set to radar in on one of three faces. Handsome faces, but that couldn't distract her from her purpose.

What was her purpose? She could do all the ranting and raving she wanted, but it more than likely wouldn't change a thing. One small, insignificant woman in a man's world. They'd probably laugh at her, like they no doubt did the last time she left their office. But she couldn't let it go. She wouldn't lie down and play dead while they took everything from her and her grandpa.

"You again." That deep, familiar voice crept under her skin, her nipples tightening in response. She whirled around, now standing in the dim central corridor of the barn.

"Colton Black. I'm surprised you have the nerve to face me after what you've done." Remembering Paddy being taken from her while she could do nothing but watch extinguished the rush of lust that had sprung to life within her. You didn't take a girl's horse.

He leaned against the wooden wall boards separating two stalls and crossed his arms over his chest. His eyes held an amused interest. "Oh? Now what have I done to upset you today, Ms. Johnson?"

She held back a growl. Ignoring him and his pompous attitude, she dashed along the length of the barn, peering in all the stalls in an attempt to find her two Quarter Horses. They had to be here.

Colton didn't move, just watched her like a man trying to understand the foolish mind of a child. She resented everything about him, especially the way he made her body betray her heart. Every time she looked at him, her blood heated, and her mouth felt dry. He must have wondered why she continually licked her lips, or why her breathing picked up to the point she had to gulp the air like a fish out of water. She could blame it on her anger and it wouldn't fully be a lie. Her anger rivaled her traitorous body.

"Looking for something, darlin'?"

She barreled toward him, leaving less than a foot separating them. Damn, the man even smelled good—a rich, musky scent mixed with the ruggedness of a cowboy. If he kept playing innocent, she wanted to be close enough to rattle him with her fists. "You know damn well what I'm looking for. You horse thief!"

"Hey! You best watch that forked tongue of yours." He gripped both her shoulders and gave her a shake, something she wasn't expecting. Why did it make her pussy throb? She fought to get away from him, but his hands were large, strong, and he seemed just as determined as she to have his own way.

"Where is he?" She nearly screamed the angry words while struggling like a rabid woman.

"Who? Your boyfriend? He's standing right over there watching you make a sorry fool of yourself."

She twisted her head in the direction of his gaze. The bay doors framed Josh's silhouette. He watched, not helping, not talking. Damn him! "Not him! My horse."

"You think I stole your horse? I own two dozen myself. What do I need with another?"

"That's what I'd like to know." When she readied her leg to kick him in the shin to gain her freedom, he tsked, leaned over, and hauled her up over his shoulder like a sack of potatoes. "Let me down! Josh, help me!"

The bastard laughed as he carried her out of the main barn to a smaller one-story structure. Josh tagged along. "Excuse me? Sir? Mr. Black? What do you intend on doing with Callie?"

"Josh! Do something!" His gentle words were no good with this hard-core cowboy.

Colton stopped briefly when Josh grabbed his arm and pulled him back. "Don't be a fool, boy. This girl will eat you for breakfast. She needs a man to teach her some manners. If you want to learn a thing or two, come along. Otherwise, get the fuck off my property."

Josh backed off and kept silent. She wanted to strangle him. Some husband he'd make. A man should defend his woman under any circumstance. She may not officially be his, but he'd made it clear on more than one occasion that he wanted a future with her.

They entered the second door in the building. A tack room. This one couldn't compare with the little room that held her equipment in the loft of her own barn. The Blacks had money, and the expensive collection of Western saddles and tack proved that. Colton unceremoniously dropped Callie to her feet.

"Close the door," he ordered Josh. After the door clicked shut, silence settled in the windowless room. The scent of leather was heavy in the air.

"What in God's name do you think you're doing?" She alternately eyed Colton and Josh. "Josh, why aren't you stopping him?"

Colton stalked forward, forcing her to awkwardly back up to the corner of the room. Her back hit the wall, and she reached both hands behind her in search of an exit or something to use as a weapon. He bore a satisfied smirk. His smoldering blue eyes focused on hers, hypnotizing her. What was he planning on doing? Surely, a wealthy rancher would be law-abiding, or in these parts, God-fearing. But he was ruthless enough to try and force her off her property and steal her horses, so she wasn't sure.

"Excuse me...sir?" Josh only stepped a foot closer to them. She saw the apprehension in his eyes as she glared at him from the side of Colton Black. Little pussy!

Colton whipped his head around. "Did I say you could interrupt me? I'm trying to teach you how to handle a woman like Callie. Isn't that what you want?"

"Yes, sir."

"Josh!" Callie stomped her foot. "Just you wait!"

Colton may have been nearly a foot taller and twice as built as Josh, but cowboys were supposed to fight for what was theirs. For God's sake, at least try.

Just then, the door burst open, knocking Josh to the side. "Oh. Sorry. I thought I heard shouting in here." Waylon stuck his head in the room and smirked when he saw how Colton had her cornered. "What's going on here?"

"I'm teaching this greenhorn how to handle a feisty filly like Callie."

"Ah, sounds like fun." He entered the room and closed the door behind him. The balance of masculine energy skyrocketed, and she could feel the testosterone practically sizzle and spark in the air around her. She felt the moisture seeping from her panties in response. Watching the hunger in the two gorgeous Black brothers' eyes made her tremble with need. Yes, she wanted them. The violent mixture of hate and lust spiraled within her, making her dizzy.

"What's your name again?" Colton asked Josh.

"Josh Evans, sir."

"How old are you? You look awful young to be tagging after her."

"Nineteen. Nearly twenty."

Waylon put his arm around the smaller man's shoulders. Josh flinched at first, like a skittish puppy. "I ain't gonna hurt you. You ever kissed a girl?"

"Yes. No, not really, sir. Well, there was—"

"Quit rambling." Waylon brushed his blond hair off his face and led Josh right beside Colton. "Kiss her."

"What!" Callie bolted back and hit her head on the wall. "You two are nuts. All three of you!"

"Go on, don't be a Betsy. Kiss her." Waylon ignored her and gave Josh a shove, forcing him forward. Josh reached both hands out to the wall on either side of Callie before landing against her. Pinned, she looked up only to see him leaning in for a kiss. She turned her head in distaste. The only reason she held a soft spot for Josh was his old-fashioned manners. Everything changed now. She didn't know who he was and felt more alone than ever. She expected no less from the Black brothers but much more from the man who had been wooing her for years.

"I think you'll have to show him how it's done, Colt." Colton nodded in agreement.

"Move aside before you shame us all." Once in front of her, Colton wrapped one arm around her waist and roughly pulled her against his body. She slammed against the firm wall of muscle his body provided. Instead of protesting, she couldn't stop thinking about what a real man Colton was, how strong, dominant. He took what he wanted and made no apologies, from property to women. No doubt he'd defend her, protect her…and win. If her grandpa wasn't on his hit list, she could see herself falling for a man like Colton Black.

When she pushed at his chest to squeeze away from his tight grip, he shook his head in disapproval, reminding her of a father scolding his daughter, and damn, did it make her hot. Her lower stomach heated and cramped. With his free hand, he tilted her chin up.

Her breathing was ragged from struggling and from the unforgivable amount of passionate energy she held for the ruffian. Why hadn't she slapped him yet? Why did the way he wet his lips make her hotter than sin? To her own surprise, she didn't turn away when he captured her mouth with his. Colton's kiss was molten lava. His lips and tongue molded to hers in a primitive, but brutal, dance. He was no gentleman but took from her greedily. She liked it.

Chapter Five

"Think you can handle that?" Colton asked the kid after pulling away from the sweetest lips he'd ever tasted.

He could see the boy's Adam's apple bob with his growing nerves. Josh would never be able to handle a woman like Callie, but he'd love the challenge himself. Unfortunately for him, she hated his guts, but that could change soon enough.

No. This was all to teach the firecracker a lesson and show the boy how to be a man.

When Josh took his place, Callie's swollen lips transformed into a straight line, and her eyes narrowed. What do you know, she preferred him over her little boyfriend. Good to know.

"Go on," Waylon encouraged.

Colton grabbed Waylon's T-shirt and pulled him back a foot to give the two lovebirds space. Callie didn't fight like he expected her to when Josh planted one right on her mouth. Within seconds, he was all hands, feeling her all over the place. Did she prefer his kiss?

As he watched, his cock grew even stiffer, making his tight jeans downright uncomfortable. Listening to her little moans of pleasure and protest did unheard-of things to his body and mind. The passion between the couple increased. When Josh reached down the front of her jeans, Colton pulled him back by the shoulder. He enjoyed watching, but that one act forced a surge of jealousy to surface that he hadn't known was even present. When he'd encouraged Josh to kiss her, he'd expected her to push him away or for the boy to bow out. After the kiss Colton had shared with her, part of him had decided he didn't want to share. He wanted more for himself.

"Cool it, cowboy. That's enough lessons for today."

"But..."

"No buts. Run along, now."

Waylon escorted him out without being told. His brother had been unusually quiet during the ordeal, and Colton wondered what he thought of the hot little number in tight blue jeans and blonde pigtail.

"I'm leaving, too," said Callie. She pushed past him toward the door in an attempt to follow Josh. Waylon slammed the door shut just before she reached it and then stood guard, trapping her alone with just Colton and his brother.

She spun around like a caged animal.

"Did you like kissing him?"

"You forced him on me. I didn't have much choice."

"No. You liked it. That tells me a lot about you."

She planted her hands on her hips. "Oh? What's that supposed to mean? Let me guess...you think I'm some cheap slut, which is why you don't give me the time of day when I come down here. I'll have you know that I'm not interested in playing your games. All I want is for you to back off, leave my grandpa's farm alone, and give me back my damn horses!"

He stepped back and raised his hands in defeat. "Never claimed you were a slut, Callie. What I was gonna say was that enjoying a kiss from that greenhorn tells me that you've never had a real man in your bed."

Her face turned a flattering pink. "Well..." she stammered. "You know nothing about me."

Colton progressed forward in slow, calculating steps. Callie countered by backing away from him. When she collided with Waylon's chest, his brother wrapped his arms around her waist in a loose embrace.

Her breathing picked up. From fear or lust, he wasn't sure. He didn't want her too scared—just a bit, so she knew who was in control. Her soft, petite body now pressed between the two men felt hot and proved a wicked temptation. Colton shared a look with Waylon over her head. They both wanted her, but since Waylon had a girlfriend, she was all Colton's.

"Give me my horses," she whispered. He could see the desire and need dancing in her big blue eyes, but her stubbornness wouldn't die easily. One of Waylon's arms traveled south until he cupped her mound through her blue jeans. She gasped from the contact, her lips parted and head nodded back against his chest. Colton took the opportunity to press into her, joining their mouths in an erotic dance. He supported her face with both hands, and after a thorough exploration of her mouth, she reached up, willingly, and pulled him closer with handfuls of his T-shirt.

"That's a good girl," he muttered against her lips.

Waylon began to unbutton and unzip her jeans from behind. Though Colton had no clue how far this party would go, he would follow it until Callie decided to end it. She had him wound up so tight, there was no way he'd be able to pull away on his own accord.

"Pull up her shirt," he told his brother. Waylon complied, pulling the cotton above her breasts. Full, youthful breasts that sloped out perfectly without the support of a bra. She had soft pink areolas that reminded him of ripe peaches. He ran his finger along the plane between her cleavage and then cupped her left breast in his hand. Ducking low, he sucked the sweet, firm bud into his mouth. Damn, the woman was perfect. Tasted perfect, too. She dug her nails into his shoulders and arched toward him. He suckled one breast, and then the other, raising the heat around them. When he released her right tit, he noticed Waylon peppering kisses up her neck to her ear. He had also weaseled his hand down the front of her open jeans.

Colton was lust-drunk, a sheen of sweat already broken out over his body. He didn't care that his brother was partaking in the woman he planned to bed. It seemed right at the moment…until she spoke.

"I'm not fucking both of you. One of you should be enough to get my land and horses back."

Her words cut through his amorous fog like a hot knife through butter. "You think I'm trying to buy your body?" He chuckled. Unbelievable. "Do you realize how many women come knocking at my door? I don't need to bribe sweet young things to get what I want. I have my pick."

"But...you're seducing me with no intention to give me back what's mine? You're using me?"

"Honey, if I had your horses, I'd give them to you. Hell, you can have one of mine." He brushed stray hairs off her face and kissed the tip of her nose. "And you'll still beg me to fuck you because you want to know what it feels like to have a real man, not a boy."

"If you're talking about Josh, he's not my boyfriend, and I've never slept with him. And as for you, if you don't have my horses, I'll be leaving!"

She straightened her shirt and lost that flirty quality that had pulled him in. It looked like he'd be sporting blue balls for a while.

* * * *

Was it wrong that she wanted Colton Black to force her to the floor and fuck her while his brother watched? The fact that he had pulled away and let her leave left her feeling empty and alone. She hadn't wanted to leave but wouldn't give him the satisfaction of letting him know that. As a matter of fact, she had no business messing around with Colton or Waylon. She had to remind herself that the Black brothers were the enemy, not potential bedmates.

Colton was right about one thing. She wanted to feel the thrill of sex with a real man. With only two sorry excuses for sexual encounters in her life, with young men who couldn't last for two minutes, she craved what Colton offered. She'd felt his cock pressing against her through his jeans—thick, hard, and ready. When sandwiched between the brothers, she'd felt their dual arousals, and the double stimulation had her senses going wild. Damn if she didn't forget about everything that ever mattered to her in those few lusty minutes.

Now, she felt like a fool. She came to the Corporation with one intention—to give the three brothers a piece of her mind and demand they return Paddy. Even now, she knew he had to be lying. Mr. McGraw said it was the Black Corporation that had forced him to sign those papers to repossess her horses. They had to be hiding the two geldings somewhere on the oversized property. If she could get away for a little while, she'd find them herself. Unfortunately, they'd worked some kind of voodoo magic on her body, making it nearly impossible to resist their advances. Yes, they were no good for her in every way.

"You sure you want to leave, sweet thing?" Colton called out from the open door she had just escaped from. She turned around only briefly in her retreat to flash him her middle finger. When she neared the open bay doors and finally finished re-buttoning her jeans, she started to jog, hoping that Josh wouldn't have left without her. He had. That no-good, sorry excuse for a man had off and left her with two maniacs. Worse yet, it was her truck that they had come in. She scanned the area, suddenly aware of all the ranch hands ogling her. If she could have become invisible, she would have. Instead, she decided that since she'd be walking home anyway, she might as well look around the property for her horses before she set off on foot. It would make her proud to catch Colton in a lie. And he had to be lying about hiring that collection agency to steal her horses.

Callie slipped behind the largest of the structures and out of sight. Each stall had its own small window that she peeked in, hoping to spot the gleaming chestnut coats of her two horses. No sign of them. Most of the horses were black Arabians, just like on the Black Corporation logo. Beautiful creatures that she'd love a chance to ride herself. The strong, sweet scent of hay both comforted and reminded her of all the work she had to do back at home. Damn those Black brothers! Once at the edge of the barn, she crouched low so she wouldn't be seen by the group of cowboys herding cattle into pens for branding. They were shouting and whistling while the tramping hooves shook the ground. They'd be too busy to notice her. She couldn't even hear her own frantic heartbeat.

Her target was the long horse barn at the other side of the pen. They had to be keeping Paddy there. But how could she get across all those cowboys without being seen?

"A cattle thief if ever I saw one."

Callie spun and fell to the ground on her bottom. Looming over her was the silhouette of a male form, complete with cowboy hat, standing in front of the strong rays of sunshine.

She scrambled to her feet and brushed off her jeans. It was Boyd, the same brother she'd blasted on her first visit. He was no less handsome than his two brothers, but while Colton and Waylon had dirty-blond hair, Boyd had deep brown waves. His body was tall and muscled like a swimmer, lean and firm and oh-so-tempting when her body still throbbed from the recent stimulation.

"A cattle thief? Ha! I'd say you're the horse thief."

"You would, would ya?"

"I know you're hiding my two horses. They were repossessed this morning by your corporation. Where are they? You had no right to pressure Mr. McGraw to sign those papers! We had an understanding."

"Darlin', you need to stop, you're making my head spin."

"I want answers!"

"Let's go find my manager, Jack Smith. He'll be able to straighten this out." He reached for her, but she jerked away.

"No way. I want nothing to do with that man."

"Colton, then."

"No. It's best if I deal with you." She couldn't handle another encounter with Colton or Waylon, not today. Her head needed to be as clear as possible to get business handled.

"Me? What do you plan on doing to me, darlin'?"

He leaned one hand against the building and moved his head closer to hers. Was that a smirk on his face? Maybe she was helpless against all three brothers, because she already felt her body responding to his nearness. Heat lashed at her, crept up her spine, and flushed her face. With a deep swallow to try and quench her dry throat, she shook her head.

"Please. Help me."

He touched her face, a light, barely-there touch with the tips of his fingers to her cheek. "Why you frettin'?"

* * * *

Boyd had been leading the branding run and had only stepped away to grab a drink of water when he'd spied Callie crouched low behind the next building. He'd prepared himself for another tongue lashing, but instead, he saw desire leap in her eyes…for him. Her chest heaved, and her slightly open mouth panted as if parched. He may have startled her, but there was definitely more.

"I—I don't know what to do. No one will help me or even be honest with me. I have nowhere to turn." The tears came next. He hadn't thought her capable of such a display of emotion. In truth, her vulnerability surprised him, and he wasn't sure how to react. Instinctively, he wrapped an arm around her slender shoulders and pulled her against his chest.

Boyd had always felt like an outsider, no matter how much his family loved him. Having been the only adopted son, he'd tried his best to accept the love surrounding him, but he'd always had that feeling of being an intruder. Their momma had thought she couldn't have children after Colton, so they adopted Boyd, only to be surprised with a miracle baby a few years later. There hadn't been a day their momma or daddy treated them differently. According to their parents, they were all blood heirs. Even his brothers treated him no differently.

There was no tangible difference, being raised as one happy family, besides the different hair color and builds.

Witnessing Callie break down brought out his protective instincts. He wanted to fix whatever wrong had been done to her and coddle her, keep the world from hurting her. It was irrational since he barely knew the girl, so he blamed it on his old-fashioned upbringing. Their father may have raised them with a strong hand, but he treated their mother like a queen.

He felt her tears penetrate his shirt. "There, there. What can I do?" He rubbed circles into her back. As the minutes passed, he noted how blonde her hair was in the sunlight and how the subtle scent of her sweet girly shampoo made his cock hard. This woman was night to day from who she'd been the other morning. Feisty arrogance versus innocent vulnerability. He had to admit he liked both sides of her. The two halves made a whole that seemed worth getting to know.

"I'm sorry. I don't know what came over me." She pulled back as quickly as she'd initially grasped for him. Wiping her eyes with the heels of her hands, she composed herself back into the tough-as-nails woman he remembered. "It's just...I have no money, I have no power, and I'm trying my darnedest to make life easier for my grandpa with no help from anyone. I thought Josh was my saving grace, but he plum left me here without a backwards glance."

"Josh? That the young one I saw barreling out of here...in your truck, I take it?"

"Yeah. Not much of a hero." She reached out and adjusted his shirt where she had crumpled it. Damn, but he wanted to be her hero. He wanted to say it out loud, too, but he buttoned his lip. Callie Johnson was trouble in a D-cup, and he had enough on his mind.

"Let's go look for this horse of yours, and you can tell me exactly what's going on, because I'm more lost than you are, sugar."

When they cut around the cattle roundup, every cowboy's eye locked onto Callie. He kept pace beside her, even bumping arms. Something primal within him felt the need to claim her, which was ridiculous. Did the ranch hands think they were together? No, probably not. Some of them would remember the spectacle she'd made on her last visit, and word spread fast, especially when a story centered around a woman as beautiful as Callie. Funny thing was he wouldn't have minded if they'd thought she was with him. In fact, he'd be proud to have a woman like her. Foolish thoughts. He knew nothing about her, only that she looked mighty fine in her Levi's. And she needed his help.

The horse barn was barren with all the hands at the roundup and branding. Hay littered the center aisle, and he could have heard a pin drop once they entered the confines of the barn. Even the horses silenced, adding to the awkwardness Boyd felt being alone with Callie. No denying he wanted her, but he also wanted to be what she needed, whatever that was.

"Go ahead. Take a look around. As far as I know, we haven't acquired any new horses lately." Callie took him up on his offer, making her way down and up the center aisle, examining some stalls longer than others. She looked all business until she returned back to where she'd started.

"They're not here." She sighed and massaged her temples with one hand to her forehead. "I better start for home. It's growing late, and I'm not getting anywhere here."

"How you gonna get home?"

"I'll walk. Ain't nothing wrong with walking." She bent down to retie her boots. "Except when someone takes your truck without permission. You don't mess with a woman's truck."

"Or her horses," he added.

Chapter Six

Callie could feel the calm authority radiating from Boyd. It comforted her, and somehow, she knew he wasn't trying to pull the wool over her eyes, even if his brothers were. He appeared genuinely interested in helping her find her horses, and after a careful search, she became more certain they weren't on the Blacks' property. Where were they? If she could pay her feed bill to Mr. McGraw, then they'd legally have to return them. But she didn't have that kind of money at the moment. She had been offering monthly payments to the feed store since she'd started sending all her extra income to the tax office. Mr. McGraw never said a word of complaint, being old friends with her grandpa.

Callie had a feeling that if she asked Boyd Black to borrow the money for her feed bill, he'd offer it without question, even barely knowing her. He was that kind of man. But she would never ask that of a stranger, of anyone.

This all had to be Colton's doing. He had that wicked gleam in his eyes, and his kiss burned hotter than hell. No, Colton was no angel, and neither was Waylon. She could imagine them doing something ruthless like using a bounty hunter to help scare her into selling her farm. Still, the ugly truth didn't diminish the primal urges flaring to life in her body when she recollected being trapped in the tack room with the two brothers. There was something about a bad boy that made her weak at the knees. But bad boys spelled trouble, and she had enough of it in her life.

Callie didn't refuse when Boyd offered to drive her home in one of the company trucks. That same rearing stallion on the logo haunted her thoughts, representing a mixture of lust and everlasting destruction.

He held the door open for her, and she quickly hopped up onto the bench. She glanced around the inside of the cab. It was the latest model truck with all the bells and whistles, nothing like her jalopy in desperate need of a new muffler. Still, the truck was hers, and she missed it. Josh Evans would be getting the worst verbal assault when she met up with him, and her truck better be parked in her lot where it should be.

"Best buckle up," he said after slipping into the driver's side. Still dazed and lost in too many thoughts, she hadn't paid enough attention to him. Boyd leaned over her to grab the seatbelt, his arm brushing her breasts as he reached up. Her nipples tightened in response, sending shivers skittering along her skin. She didn't have time to stop the throaty gasp that escaped her throat from the contact.

They met eyes, so close. She could feel his breath, see his chest expanding, and smell his masculine cologne. He was certainly a handsome man. With his strong jawline, straight nose, and squinty eyes the color of sapphires, he presented himself as an overwhelming temptation. How would his kiss compare to his brothers'? She imagined Boyd would savor her—tasting, exploring—while Colton took without apology, ravishing her with his erotic brutality.

Sometimes, she craved sex as an excuse for the comfort and companionship she desperately needed. She could pretend for those few minutes that a man truly cared for her. A momentary escape from her crippling reality was tempting. But Boyd was a Black and spelled trouble by association.

The seatbelt clicked into place, and Boyd pulled away, keeping his eyes locked with hers. He took a cleansing breath and started his truck, extinguishing any lusty thoughts she held for him. Callie turned to look out the passenger window at the many familiar sights of farm life. As they pulled onto the driveway, she saw Colton step out of the barn and lean against the frame, watching the truck depart. Her heart sped up just seeing him, and she cursed herself for being so affected by the sexy bastard.

"You don't have to do this," she repeated.

"I told you, it's no trouble." His voice was husky, and he spoke in such an unrushed manner, reminding her of her grandpa's old-fashioned ways. Nothing about him was hurried, even the smooth way he shifted gears. She imagined he'd remain calm even in the face of a life-threatening emergency. How would he react to her lips around his cock? Would he maintain his integrity or finally lose control? She craved to see him sweat-glistened and begging.

Callie shook her head, not sure what to blame her off-the-chart hormone levels on. First Colton and Waylon, now Boyd. Was there something unique to the Black brothers that made her lust-crazy?

As they traveled toward her farm, every dip in the road jolted her and made her pussy throb. She stole glances at the cowboy beside her. Strong thighs fit snuggly in his blue jeans, and the shirt rolled up to his elbows revealed thick, muscled forearms. She had to resist the urge to lay her hand over his, so strong and masculine, gripping the stick shift.

"Are you close with your brothers?" Her mind begged for a reason the three brothers seemed so different.

"Sure."

Not much of an answer. "Did you find out anything from your manager about my farm?"

He cleared his throat and gave her a quick sideways glance. "Sorry. No. Things have been busy lately. We're in the middle of an expansion plan."

"I'd appreciate it if you'd look into it. My entire future is at stake here, as well as my grandpa's."

"I'll do that. See if Jack knows anything about your horses, too."

* * * *

When they arrived at Callie's property, Boyd stopped short of the gravel drive. This was his chance. If he let Callie out the door without trying to make a connection, he'd regret it for the rest of his life. There was fire in her eyes for him, whether she admitted it or not. She had no ring on her finger, and the guy who'd driven her to their ranch had deserted her. That left her up for grabs.

She may have given him a tongue lashing the first time they met, but she'd had her reasons. Things were different now. The spitfire calmed, and he felt a connection between them. His urge to help her, to comfort her, was a new instinct for him. Women rarely got under his skin, and he didn't do long-term relationships.

"Why we stopping?" she asked.

Because I want to take you right here in the cab. "Thought we could talk for a minute."

"Okay…" She crossed her arms over her chest and twisted to face him. "What do you want to talk about?"

"First, you should never cross your arms like that." He shifted closer, sliding along the leather upholstered bench, and unfolded her arms. With his hands still locked loosely around her thin wrists, he continued. "It's rude."

"Is it now?" Her demeanor soured. "Don't you think it's rude for wealthy men to run small farmers off their land? Land that's been in their families for generations?"

"Callie," he whispered. "I'm not the bad guy."

She wet her pretty pink lips and just stared. He expected some smart-aleck retort, but she kept quiet. Only the sound of wind passing through wheat fields coming from the open windows could be heard.

"What are you, then? Are you my knight in shining armor? Are you going to take my nightmares away?" Her sarcastic tone cut him down a notch because he wanted to connect with her. He felt something between them. Couldn't she?

"If you let me." He released one wrist and gently ran his fingers along her jawline. Her skin was as soft and feminine as he'd imagined. She took in a small, sharp breath before swallowing hard.

"Boyd." She started to lean into his touch but pulled back. "I can't do this." Callie shook her head, and he felt her pulling away emotionally, like water through his fingers. "You're a Black. Until I find out what's going on with the farm and my horses, I just can't."

"I promise you. I'm not out to steal your farm. I'll get this all sorted out."

She opened the door and hopped out faster than he could snatch her back. "Well, until you do, I'll be keeping my distance. I expect you to do the same, Mr. Black."

There was no arguing with the feisty vixen. He would have driven her up the long drive, but she took off at a steady clip toward the little bungalow in the distance. His first thought, besides his painful hard-on, was getting to the bottom of the land issue so he'd have an excuse to see Callie again. There was something there worth pursuing. He'd never felt so worked up about a woman before.

* * * *

Boyd spread the large map out on the conference table as his two brothers, Jack Smith, and Mary Sue looked on.

"There." He pointed to the Johnson property. "This is the land she says we're trying to purchase. Anyone have a clue?"

"I don't know, but you fellas better hurry up and find out. The next time that little number comes storming in, she's liable to skin the three of you alive." Mary Sue shook her head. Their secretary was like a second mother to Boyd and his brothers. She had worked for their father when they were just young ones, so she had a place in many of their childhood memories.

"No shit," said Colton. "I'd like her to pay a visit when she's less pissed off." He shot Waylon a mischievous grin, and Boyd didn't like it one bit. If he knew his brothers, and he did, he had to act fast, or one of them would take Callie for himself. Maybe both of them. The women couldn't seem to resist their cowboy charms, and they often worked as a team, something Boyd was never interested in, even though they tried to get him to join them.

Boyd tried to remain focused despite his rising irritation. "Jack, do you know anything about this? The property or the horses?"

Jack slipped out a pair of prescription glasses from his front breast pocket and carefully placed them over his nose, leaning over the table to inspect the map. "Hmmm. I know we've been looking at potential properties for the growth and restructuring plan. These four properties in red," he waved his hand over the area in question, "we need them to expand the ranch. We talked about this numerous times, Boyd. You knew it was essential to buy more real estate if we were to build your family business to the point you hoped to take it."

Boyd scratched his head. "Yeah, but isn't there anything we can do? Maybe buy from the east instead?" He knew the river to the east would make the idea impossible, but he hoped there would be another way. Disappointing Callie was not something he looked forward to.

"Boyd. We've been through this. You knew exactly what we were planning, and that property is dead center where we need to take our restructuring."

Boyd dropped heavily into the nearest chair. It felt like a vise grip had wrapped itself around his chest. "I know. I just didn't think about the human cost. Callie Johnson and her grandfather don't deserve to be run off their land because we want to expand."

Jack slammed a fist on the table, startling him and rattling the ice in Colton's iced tea. "She's got you brainwashed now! Some spoiled little princess shows up wiggling her ass, and you fall right into her charms. Wake up, boy! She's a siren, trying to play you for a fool and all you're worth."

Boyd looked to Colton and Waylon. His youngest brother only shrugged. Colton's face weathered in discernable conflict. "You sure there ain't another way around this mess?" asked Colton.

Jack's heated glare was his answer.

"Great. I promised her I'd make things right. I don't like being made a liar." Boyd stood, rising well above the irritated manager, and folded the map into its original form.

Chapter Seven

Callie pulled a wooden peg from her mouth and clipped it on the line over a large white sheet. The material fluttered in the slight breeze, sending the fresh soapy scent across the fields. She had a mountain of laundry to dry and a lengthy list of chores to be attended to. With her mind elsewhere the past few days, she'd been slacking, and it was time to get back to reality. She was still playing normal with her grandpa, so she couldn't sulk or stare at the walls forever without him growing suspicious. Life had to go on, no matter how difficult.

She carefully stepped off the stepladder and pulled another damp article from her overflowing basket. As she stood up, her peripheral vision caught movement out in the fields where it didn't belong. Dropping the clothes back in the pile, she stood straight and stared as two horses came galloping toward her house. Her first instinct was to run off and secure her rifle from the barn, but as the figures approached, the sleek black horses reminded her of something she desperately tried to forget every day. The Black brothers.

Callie straightened her shirt and tucked her loose hair behind her ears. Why did she care what she looked like? Why did her heart race a mile a minute in anticipation? Never had a man made her feel so virile, so alive. Now three had managed it effortlessly.

The horses slowed to a trot, and the two cowboys dismounted before they came to a full stop. Waylon dipped his hat, gave her a roguish grin, and led his horse to her barn as if he owned the place. Colton smacked his stallion on the rump, and it followed Waylon obediently. Hah! Paddy was the best trained horse she'd ever seen and would put any of Colton's animals to shame.

"What's this about? I hope you came to tell me that you've given up trying to steal my property." Callie planted her hands on her hips and tried to act as authoritative as possible, considering her stomach fluttered with need just looking at the masculine temptation. Colton's dirty-blond hair was slightly matted to his head when he removed his hat, but a quick comb-through with his fingers left him rugged and too handsome to be holy. He devoured her with his ocean-blue eyes, even though she had nothing on but faded jeans and a plain white T-shirt. Still, there was no denying his need as he closed the space between them. He licked his lips and tilted her chin up with a bent finger.

"We have a little proposition for you," he drawled. The deep timbre of his voice sent shivers racing down her spine. She hid her desire well, scowling and pulling away from his touch when she wanted nothing more than to lean into his chest and inhale his masculine scent.

"A proposition? Okay, let's hear it." What did she have to lose? She'd do just about anything to save her grandpa's farm. Callie expected they'd ask her to parcel off her land and sell them what they needed. Heck, she'd even sell it if they'd let her rent the land. Her grandfather wouldn't be around forever. Once he was gone, they could have whatever they wanted, but not a second before.

"Waylon's waiting for us in the barn. I'll let him tell you."

She glared at him. The mysterious way he spoke and the subtle hint of a smirk made her leery at best. She had little choice but to follow him. He appraised her land as he walked, looking side to side, and she wondered if he planned his takeover or only judged the simplicity of her way of life in comparison to his.

"I suppose you don't have to hang your clothes to dry," she said with disdain.

"Why wouldn't I?"

"Don't tell me you live without electric dryers and every other luxury gadget known to man."

"Maybe. But I don't have a wife or mother to take care of me." He walked backwards now, awaiting her reaction. She may have felt a foreign instinct to care for him, be the woman he needed in one weak moment, but she brushed it away. He was an egocentric pig like the lot of them.

"Is that all women are good for? Cooking and cleaning? I should have expected as much from you." Callie pushed past him and entered the dim interior of her century barn. It may have been old, but it was well maintained. She bet it would be standing another hundred years from now...if the Blacks didn't get their paws on it first.

"Where's your brother?" she muttered, looking around the empty space.

"Boo!" Waylon jumped out from behind her, hidden in a dark stall, and pinched her sides. She squealed and whirled around. Both men converged on her, and all those feelings from a few days earlier came to the surface. Her panties grew moist, and her womb coiled tight. With her body crying out to be fucked, she was fighting a losing battle.

"What's your proposition?" Business. She had to talk business before she lost her mind completely. The heat from their bodies mingled with hers in the limited space separating them. It didn't help that she knew exactly what it felt like to be sandwiched between them, their hard cocks pressed against her body.

Colton circled her, but she didn't turn fully around to monitor his movements because Waylon remained in front of her. She felt like she was being sized up for the kill. Not being able to watch them both at the same time left her feeling vulnerable and fidgety.

"We might be willing to make a trade," said Waylon. As he chewed on a piece of straw, his perfect lips looked edible. Both brothers were too relaxed and cocky, while she felt uncomfortable in her own skin being near them.

"A trade?"

"What would you be willing to do to save your farm?"

"Anything," she blurted. The resulting smile appearing on Waylon's face made her regret her quick response. She swallowed hard as he leaned against the narrow wooden planks between two empty stalls and raked his gaze over her body. Slowly. She could feel it. Every place his eyes met heated with erotic intensity, like a physical caress roaming her body.

"Take off your clothes."

"What!" She spun around to find Colton. He looked quite comfortable sitting back on a bale of hay, fiddling with a length of rope he'd found. "Did you hear him?" she asked in disbelief.

"I'd do as he says if you care about your farm, darlin'."

"You can't be serious. I'm not taking off my clothes." She hugged herself, not knowing where to begin her verbal tirade. They actually looked serious. "Women may sell themselves to you whenever you ask, but I won't. I'm no whore!"

"Never said you were, Callie. It's only business. You want something. We want something." Waylon tossed the piece of straw and pushed off from the wall. "Now, are you in, or are you out?"

"This is ridiculous." She looked Waylon right in the eyes, pleading, hoping there was some shred of decency in the man. "You're actually going to force me to fuck you?"

"Of course not," said Colton from behind. She twisted and backed up so she could see them both. The situation had her feeling like a caged rat, desperate to escape. "You're going to fuck both of us. And you'll do it willingly."

Callie opened her mouth to speak, but for once, she was speechless. The shock of their arrogance left her stunned and seriously turned on. Liquid heat seeped in her panties, making her desperate to rub her legs together to create friction. Everything felt so wrong, but she'd also never wanted anything more. Would she actually go through with their offer to save her farm? She always believed she'd do anything for her grandpa's health and happiness. Callie supposed this was the ultimate test of that love.

Still standing in silence, Colton broke the hush. "I think Waylon asked you do something, sweet thing."

Jaw slack, she met Waylon's gaze. "The clothes. Off."

Her heart began pumping wildly. She wasn't a virgin, but it had been a long time since she'd had a man, and the men she'd had could barely be called men. The two in front of her were all male, prepared for a full cowboy domination of her body. First her property, then her horses, now her very soul?

"Darlin', don't tell me you need punishment already. I've been branding cattle all day, but I still have the energy to leave my mark on your sweet little ass." Colton spoke to his brother next. "Help her out of those clothes."

Waylon complied, moving his hard body against hers and snaring the hem of her shirt as she backed away from him. Her back hit the wall, and he ground his steely cock into her stomach and forced her shirt over her head with little effort. The excitement of being taken without permission had her panting and rearing to go. No way would she give them the satisfaction of knowing how eager she was to participate in their lewd acts, though. She was no whore.

His hands dipped lower and began to unclasp her jeans and pull down the zipper. Her breath caught as the reality of her situation became more than evident. She couldn't do this…but she wasn't stopping Waylon, either.

As he bent and attempted to tug her jeans down her rounded hips, she gripped his shoulders for balance. She sighed inwardly at the strength and firmness of his muscles. "Take your shirt off, too. It's only fair," she whispered. The request felt too bold, too willing, but she had to feel his man-flesh against her fingers.

He didn't linger but complied immediately, standing and pulling his shirt off over his head, dropping it beside him. Without thought, she reached out and trailed her fingertips along the defined ripples over his stomach, reveling in the feel of him. She crept up to his firm pecs and massaged her hands over the thick muscles, feeling his small brown nipples become rigid under her palms.

"You're beautiful, Callie." He dropped low and nuzzled her neck. His heated breath stimulated her already heightened senses. "I can't wait to get inside you." Waylon trailed soft, barely there kisses up the side of her neck as he unfastened her bra with ease. As soon as her breasts were free of their restraint, he reached for them, measuring their weight in his hands.

"Waylon, move aside," said Colton from his perch on the hay bales.

When Waylon stepped to the side, exposing her nude breasts to his brother, her nipples tightened instantly, and her pussy clenched. The way those penetrating blue eyes assessed her turned her feral. She wanted him touching her, tasting her, along with Waylon. Not just watching.

"Your body was made to be loved, darlin'. I've been dreaming about those tits of yours since you showed up at the ranch braless."

"Go let Colton touch you," said Waylon, prodding her toward his brother. The way they shared her, like some toy, was bizarre.

She walked forward like a programmed robot, the breeze from the open bay doors tickling her naked flesh. Colton held out his arms, and as soon as she was close enough, he tugged her closer with a hand to each side of her waist. She dropped a knee on the hay bale between his parted legs to avoid falling. Before she knew what was happening, his mouth was covering her areola. He suckled her, and she found herself arching into him, wanting more. Every pull on her sensitive nipples sent pleasure skittering through every inch of her body, relaxing her, making her forget right and wrong. Like a drug released into her system, she no longer fought the invasion but accepted it, wanted it. If this was her task to get the farm back, she might as well enjoy herself.

Chapter Eight

Colton and Waylon often took turns dominating the women they took to bed, but today, Colton had no intentions of giving up control to his youngest brother. He wanted to make his little spitfire obey, to douse some of that unwanted temper into compliance. The lust dancing in her eyes as he devoured her soft, full breasts told him the task would be easier than expected. He loved a full bosom on a petite woman—nothing was sexier. Callie was all natural, perfect, and she tempted him like no other. His cock strained painfully in his jeans. Colton had to fight the crippling urge to press her to the hay-littered floor and fuck her hard and mercilessly. But no, he wanted to enjoy every second of this seduction, this erotic dance he knew too well.

"The pants, Waylon." Colton called the shots, but Waylon would be his voice, the middleman in this sexual game.

"Callie, pull down your pants. Face Colton, and drop them to your ankles."

She didn't talk back, just did as she was told, which only made his cock harder. With a final wiggle, she kicked off her shoes and danced out of her pants without using her hands. Her panties were white and cotton. He'd have to change that, buy her some expensive lace bits. She'd look amazing in the lingerie he envisioned her wearing.

"You're wet, Callie. Your panties look soaked through." She reached down and touched herself, almost making him lose his sanity. It was a picture that would be engrained in his memory for some time to come.

"It's hot out," she said.

"No. You're wet because you want to be fucked. Be a good girl and unbuckle me." Colton leaned back farther, clasping his hands behind his head as a makeshift pillow.

She stood still, her eyes wide.

"You heard him, Callie. Undo his belt, unzip him, and pull out his cock." His brother was so good at this game. Judging by the bulge in his jeans, he enjoyed it as much as Colton.

Callie squatted down beside him, her breasts crushing against his thigh as she undid the thick leather belt from his jeans. Her slender fingers moved with grace, slowly, cautiously. She never looked him in the eyes, just did as she was asked.

"That's it," said Waylon once the zipper was pulled low. "Now reach in and release his cock." She obeyed, her small hand gripping his erection and freeing it from the confines of his pants. He groaned at the freedom and the feel of her hand caressing his sensitive flesh. A bead of pre-cum glistened at the tip of his thick head. He'd never been harder and more desperate than now.

"Waylon, you're torturing me." Colton groaned, tempted to grab Callie's head and pull it to his throbbing member—but that would break the rules.

"Callie, do you like Colton's cock? Big enough for you?"

She turned her head to Waylon, her face slightly pale, no doubt from shock. Callie may have a smart mouth, but she was pure innocence compared to the women they usually played with. She nodded briefly.

"Good girl. Now I want you to take a taste. Lick the head of Colton's cock with that wicked tongue of yours." She pursed her lips and appeared ready to argue, but instead, she leaned over his lap and tentatively lapped at the pre-cum rolling down the side of his mushroom head. The electric current shot straight to his balls, which tightened up against his body. He'd have to concentrate not to spew his load before the game even began. He and Waylon planned to double-team the sweet filly and show her how a woman should be pleasured.

Though Waylon had only told her to take a taste, she didn't stop there. Her tongue painted erotic patterns around his swollen head. He could see her chest heaving from labored breathing, her eyes sparkling with undiluted lust. When she wrapped her lips around his cock and sucked deeply, he thought he'd die from the pleasure of it.

"Fuck! That tongue is put to much better use on my dick." The first day he'd spotted her cursing out Boyd, he'd imagined she'd be a fiery lover, and it appeared he was right in his assumption. She knew how to tease him, sucking and rolling her tongue around the acorn ridge of his cock, making him shudder.

"Callie, I said take a taste, not indulge in a meal. I know you're hungry, darlin', but you have to learn to obey." Waylon stepped closer and knelt down on one knee beside Callie. Waylon tilted her head toward him, her hand still wrapped around Colton's throbbing length, and stole a kiss. Colton watched as their tongues danced and mingled together. Within seconds, his brother had her under his spell. She forgot his erection and wrapped her arms up around Waylon's neck, deepening their kiss.

He knew Waylon was being generous because of Callie's innocence, but it was even more than that. Waylon looked at her the same way Colton did, with adoration. He supposed they wanted more from her than this one night, but that was still to be seen.

Waylon pulled his head back, leaving Callie panting for more. "Okay, sweetheart, take off them panties and lie down on the ground." He stood and grabbed one of the rust-colored saddle blankets off a sawhorse and spread it on the concrete floor of the barn. She rose out of her crouch and looked to each of them in turn, her eyes lingering over Colton's erection.

Before removing her panties, she sat on the blanket, wiggling about to get comfortable, and then shimmied out of her undergarment. Once her body was gloriously naked in the open space of the barn, he couldn't help but stroke his shaft. She looked like an angel, pale skin, blonde hair, and baby-blue eyes that could melt even the strongest man's heart. He wasn't sure if he was immune to her charms himself. Every minute that passed made him more desperate to fuck her. But was this just about sexual gratification or something more?

"That's perfect, Callie. Now lie back, bend your knees, and spread your legs wide for me." She lay back on command but hesitated in opening her legs for their inspection. "Come on, now. Don't make me do it for you," warned Waylon.

Ever so slowly, her legs parted, revealing her glistening pink pussy with a neatly trimmed runway of dark blonde hair. "Beautiful," Colton muttered before he could stop himself.

Waylon maintained control, giving him a heated glare. "Now I want you to touch yourself. Be a good girl, and touch your clit." She reached her hand low and massaged soft circles into the engorged nub, so ripe for the picking. "Now I want you to take two fingers and push them in your pussy. Come on, darlin', fuck yourself for us."

Callie parted her folds with her fingers and plunged into the sweet nectar-filled recesses that he desperately wanted to explore for himself. She dropped her head back and made soft mewling sounds filled with desire and need.

* * * *

Waylon was on his own for this show. His brother had lost it early on, and if they wanted to maintain control, he'd have to be the one to ensure it. He'd never seen Colton so out of his wits for a woman. Always the womanizer, never without his bravado, Waylon didn't recognize his brother. This fantasy would be short-lived because Colton wouldn't last much longer.

"You're such a good listener, Callie. Such a good girl. Let's see just how behaved you are." Waylon made his way to the stall he'd tied his horse in and flipped open the leather of his saddlebag. A treasure trove of adult toys stared back at him, and he couldn't help but smile as he imagined using them on the buxom blonde writhing on the floor of the barn. Her moans were increasing by the second, and he didn't want her to orgasm until he gave her permission. For now, he grabbed his sleek tube of lube and a silicone dildo. The vibrating toys would come later.

As soon as he reappeared outside the stall, he found his brother's face buried deep in Callie's pussy. "Fuck, Colton!" He nudged his brother's shoulder with his boot to remove him. This wasn't part of the plan, but the source of his brother's attention sure enjoyed the treat. She clawed at the saddle blanket and arched her hips up to meet Colton's mouth. When he pulled away, she groaned and writhed with impatience.

"I have something for you, cupcake. You'll like this." He drizzled some lube on the end of the red phallus and dropped to his knees. "Hold her legs open," he told Colton. The woman couldn't lie still, rubbing her legs together and twisting about almost painfully. How long had it been since she'd had a man? Her breasts jiggled, her nipples firm buds. Once her legs were spread wide, he prodded her moist folds with the toy and wedged it into her tight pussy with some difficulty. The lube helped, but the girl was tight as a fist, and he couldn't wait to plant his own dick deep inside her.

She reached both hands to the dildo, but he swatted her away and began to thrust the silicone in and out of her body. "Hold her arms up, she's being naughty."

With Colton holding her arms back, Waylon leaned between her legs to hold her thighs apart and fucked her with the dildo. The little vixen fought while continuing to kiss his brother. Erotic squeals filled the hollow interior of the barn, making his erection painfully hard.

"Callie, are you gonna behave for me while I try something new?"

She nodded eagerly, her swollen lips parted, arms still pinned above her head. Not once had she spoken since she'd asked him to lose his shirt. He applied more lube to the silicone dick and twirled the head around her nether hole, that tight, dark rosebud begging to be explored. This invasion would not come nearly as easily as it had with her pussy.

She pressed her legs together with a gasp. "Colton, get the rope, this filly needs to be broke."

Chapter Nine

Callie's entire body was on fire with a heat that warmed from the inside out. Her pussy had a pulse of its own, strong and demanding. What kind of sweet torture was this? She wanted to be dirty. Wanted to be fucked by both cowboys. What was wrong with her? They cast their lusty spell on her, and she was helpless to resist it.

"This wouldn't be necessary if Boyd were here. He could hold her legs while I hold her arms," said Colton.

"You know he ain't interested in our games. Tie her ankles. You can hold her arms after."

Callie lay on the cool ground, watching and listening. She was their puppet and eager to receive the pleasure they planned to give her. When Waylon had pumped the cool plastic toy in her body, she couldn't help but crave the real thing—a hot, hard length of male flesh.

Colton secured her own rope around each ankle, anchoring them to posts at each side of the barn. The vulnerability of being so exposed oddly turned her on. Anyone who walked through those bay doors would look straight up her cunt, and just the idea had moisture trickling from her pussy to her ass like a lazy river of liquid heat. Callie tested her bindings once Colton stood. No way was she going anywhere with her legs so secure.

"That's perfect. Now you can't impede my exploration of your sweet little ass."

Right. He had tried to enter her virginal entrance with the toy and failed. The act had adrenaline shooting through her body in a mixture of nerves and erotic need. Would he actually force that big red dick into her ass when she was completely unable to fight him off? God, she hoped so.

Colton's thighs straddled her head from behind as he held her wrists snuggly in his lap so she couldn't resist Waylon's ministration. "I'm scared," she whimpered, barely a whisper. Would they even care? They'd asked her to trade her body for her farm. This was just sex, and they'd have no pity on her until they'd had their perverted lust filled.

"Just relax, Callie." Colton leaned forward and plucked her nipple gently with his teeth, making her gasp. Next came his tongue, hot and skilled, before he sucked her breast, his stubble tickling her fleshy mounds.

As one brother lavished her breasts, the other proceeded with trying to deflower her ass. She clenched tight automatically, fearing the unknown.

"Don't tighten up on me, sugar." Waylon massaged her clit with one hand, successfully loosening up her coiled body, while prodding her forbidden entrance with the slick toy. At first, he wiggled it, twisting it back and forth, wedging it in. When it popped in past her unforgiving anal ring, she cried out at the burst of unexpected pain. A pain mixed with a sinful pleasure. "That's a girl. Relax. You're doing great." Waylon lowered his head and sucked on her sensitive nub while pushing the fake cock deeper in measured increments. The multitude of sensations wracking her body pulled her waiting orgasm to just below the surface. Colton sucked her breasts hard, alternating from one to the other, never freeing her arms. Waylon fucked her ass with the dildo while sucking her pussy with an inhuman hunger.

Once the toy was fully seated in her nether hole, the unusual fullness carried a new sensation that she grew to like more with every passing moment. But she wanted more. She wanted both Waylon and Colton naked and fucking her. No toys. Why were they torturing her?

Being vulnerable, not having to worry about being in charge or competing in a man's world, felt liberating. She gave herself up, body and mind, somehow trusting the Black brothers not to hurt her.

In a rush of heat and a rainbow of color, her orgasm burst forth, taking her by surprise. Never had she felt anything so intense, so incredible. Her ass milked the toy, and Waylon sucked her pussy until her tremors finally eased away, leaving her a boneless mass.

"Just so you know, next time you come without being told, you'll be punished."

"What're you gonna do? Tie me up?" she asked.

"You have no idea, darlin'. I'd love to see your lily-white ass red and throbbing from a good spanking."

Callie scowled at Waylon. He wouldn't dare. Would he? Before she got to experience whatever they had in store for her next, she heard a truck door slam shut. Panic zinged through her, and she kicked at her ankle restraints, desperate to conceal her nudity and the lewd act she was partaking in.

"Get rid of whoever it is," said Colton, not moving. He released her wrists and used one hand to her shoulder to keep her down, while tenderly brushing her sweat-slick hair off her face with the other. Funny how such a simple act could warm her heart, make her feel loved. Waylon stood and sauntered to the bay doors, shirtless, not a care in the world. When he reached the end, the sun highlighted his blond hair and golden skin, beginning a new wave of desire deep in her core. With the dildo still inside her ass, every time she clamped down on it, erotic thrills cascaded throughout her lower body.

"Jack? What are you doing out here?"

"Came to deliver the seven-day eviction notice personally."

"We need to talk about that, Jack."

"Oh, really? And I suppose I can guess why you're here. Colton here, too?" Callie heard footsteps over the gravel coming closer to the entrance of the barn.

"Let me free. He'll see me!" she whispered harshly. Colton growled as he stood. He went to join Waylon, ignoring her plea for release.

"Ah hah. I should have known. That siren has you both hooked now, same as your brother, Boyd. Do you want to be a midsized operation forever, or do you want to be known as a big-time cattle ranch?" There was a silent pause. Neither Waylon nor Colton disputed him. "Where is Ms. Johnson at, anyway? She claimed she'd have the money to pay her back taxes, but with only a week left, I seriously doubt that's possible."

"She's tied up at the moment." Didn't she know it. She sat up and unfastened the tight knots at her ankles, freeing her outstretched legs. It felt good to move her limbs and flex her strained muscles. She gasped when she pulled the red cock out of her ass, dropping it to the ground, where it rolled in the hay. Struggling to dress herself as quickly as possible, she donned her jeans, shirt, and boots, ignoring her undergarments, before pulling and twisting her hair into a makeshift bun.

She stormed out of the barn, ready to raise hell if need be. "Mr. Smith, as far as I'm aware, I still have a week before you can set foot on my property."

"Just delivering your court-ordered eviction notice." His smile was devilish, and she wanted to smack it off his face. Could he see the recent orgasm still flush on her cheeks?

"Which is no good for another week."

"Well, I don't see things changing in your favor anytime soon. Do you?"

"Get off my land." He smirked, tossed her the envelope, and turned back toward his truck. "And just so you know, I'll be leaving my dogs out at night, and they don't care for strangers."

"I'd bridle and brand that one if I were you, boys. She needs an attitude adjustment."

"Off!" she shouted. Her dogs were clawing at the shed door, growling louder as they sensed her growing irritation. She had a mind to let the three beasts loose to teach Mr. Jack Smith a lesson he'd never forget. But with her luck, he'd have the sheriff come and charge her.

She watched as he reversed, turned, and pulled out of her long driveway in a company vehicle, leaving a spray of gravel in its wake. Once out of sight, she exhaled a long, drawn-out breath. Eviction notice? She whirled around and pressed an accusing finger in each cowboy's chest. "You both told me that we had a deal! If I played the whore for the afternoon, you'd ensure I had my farm back." Her voice was loud, ragged, and edging on hysterical. She'd done unspeakable things with these men in the barn, and for what? They'd take her farm anyway? Did they know this from the beginning?

"Now, now, Callie Lynn," said Waylon, reaching to steady her by the shoulders as if she may erupt. Maybe she would.

"Don't call me that! Only my grandpa calls me that name. You have no right." Tears pricked at her eyes, and she hated that these men affected her so strongly. "There never was a deal was there? You never intended to give me back my farm."

"Callie," Colton pleaded. "It's not like that."

She let out a half-growl, half-scream and stomped her foot. "Get off my land. Take your horses and go!" She pointed to the barn, not looking them in the eyes. Her heart beat wildly in her chest, half broken, half humiliated. She'd never let on that they affected her emotionally. They'd only ever see her anger from now on. Screw submission!

* * * *

Colton didn't bother to argue with Callie in her livid state. Jack's timing had been impeccable. The man was never around when you wanted him and always showed up at the wrong time. Colton and

Waylon had been so close to subduing Callie, and now all their fantasies were shattered.

He unfastened his horse and led him out of the barn. Callie stood in the same spot, arms crossed, foot tapping to an angry beat. She looked like an angel scorned. Would she ever give them a second chance? He doubted it and didn't deserve any better. They had no plans to give her back her land, but since it was obvious she had wanted them when back on their ranch in the tack room, they thought an ultimatum would give her the permission she needed to let loose. No, he didn't want her farm, but progress was progress. They hired Jack to help them expand their operation so they could compete with the big boys. One small casualty wasn't worth throwing away months of research and money, according to Jack Smith. Colton wasn't so sure. He wanted to live up to his father's legend, but he wasn't his father, only playing the part as the eldest.

After hooking one foot in the stirrup, he swung up onto his horse and sidled up to Callie. "It ain't like you think."

"You've already said that. Go!"

With a tug of the reins and a soft heel to the horse's side, he galloped off after Waylon. He'd say coming was a mistake, but the only thing he regretted was not being able to finish what they started. Maybe more. He began to see his brother Boyd's determination to help the young thing. The thought of her losing her farm, becoming broken and blaming, made his head hurt. He wasn't good at this. Being a bachelor, living the good life, didn't have consequences and repercussions. When you didn't give a shit about the women you fucked, you could maintain a clear conscience.

But Callie wasn't like his other women. She was pure, sweet, a cowgirl with spunk, with a body to die for. The others he'd had in the past, alone or with Waylon, knew what they were getting into. Not a one cared about them, only desired their bodies, status, or money. Callie wanted to save her grandfather's farm. Otherwise, he doubted she'd touch them with a ten-foot pole under the circumstances.

Guilt began to rise up in his chest, constricting his breathing. He should never have tricked her. Shit. If he wanted something real with Callie, he should have taken the time to court her proper. What was wrong with him? She made him crazy, lust drunk, and stupid. All he could think about was getting her naked and under him.

Colton slowed to a trot as they neared their ranch. Waylon pulled up alongside him.

"That went well."

"I told you I never liked that Jack fella."

"It's for the best. We never should have tricked her like that."

Waylon only shrugged and clicked his tongue for his horse to continue on ahead. When he needed to talk, to spill his guts, he didn't turn to his brothers or even his parents. It was time to visit Mary Sue.

* * * *

Callie kicked her basket of damp laundry, spilling the contents all over the dirt-laden ground, soiling the lot. She didn't care. Those bastards used her like some cheap whore. It was bad enough she'd agreed to trade her body for the farm. But for nothing? She growled and searched for something to throw or kick. When she was tucked up in her bed at night, she'd no doubt feel sorry for herself, cry pointless tears, and end up harder than when she'd started. Now she was pissed off.

Her temper was her weakness. She knew she had control issues. Right now, she felt like grabbing her rifle, hopping in her truck, and visiting those Blacks just to blast off their balls. Of course, those were fantasies. She'd never do anything so foolish.

Seven days. She had seven days to pay off her back taxes, or the Blacks would get everything she owned. Her grandfather would no doubt fall more ill, and worse than that, he'd have a broken heart. Where could she turn? She had nobody in the world. Josh had always been there to lend a hand, but he'd shown his true colors, the yellow-bellied weasel. It was all up to her. The only thing she could do now was start selling. She'd sell every last head of cattle, parcel off and rent some of the land, even get a night job waitressing at the Hoe Down. God, she felt so small having to stoop to such levels. But she had no choice. Holding her shoulders back, she marched to her truck. Her destination—the Black ranch.

Chapter Ten

She fought the urge to turn around the entire trip. Crawling back with your tail between your legs never felt good. But her pride and honor had to be put aside for her grandfather's happiness.

Inside the lobby of the office, the secretary who usually sat at the desk was absent. Once the glass door sealed shut behind her, an uncomfortable silence settled in. "Hello?" she called out, her voice echoing.

After two more shouts, she heard rummaging coming from down the hall, then footsteps. "Ms. Johnson, I wasn't expecting to find you here. I thought you were still back on your ranch entertaining the Black brothers." She ground her molars together to keep from cussing him out. He had that filthy little smirk that made her feel cheap and little.

"I've come to talk business, Mr. Smith. I have sixty head of cattle. In today's market, they should cover three quarters of my back taxes. I'll raise the rest myself."

"Give it up, little lady." He adjusted his belt. "You can't win. If you pay now, there will be more bills the next month, and with no cattle, how do you expect to earn an income?"

"I can work. I'll get a job at the Hoe Down."

"*Tsk tsk tsk.* You know what kind of women work down there?" He licked his lips. "Easy women. Women who can be bought and sold like cattle." He tucked some loose hair behind her ear. "Are you easy, Ms. Johnson? Think I can buy a piece of you?"

"You best watch your mouth, Mr. Smith. I came here to talk business." She stepped back.

"So am I. Unlike Waylon and Colton Black, I keep my word. They promised you things they knew they couldn't provide. I can." His words affected her because she wanted to believe the brothers. Damn those Blacks for toying with her emotions.

"And what exactly is it that you want?"

He closed his eyes and took a deep breath. When he exhaled, the air smelled like cold cuts. She grimaced and stepped farther back, but he hooked an arm around her waist and tugged her against his body.

"Why don't we go into my office and see what we can arrange." His words were heavy with a twisted desire that she wanted no part in. She may have agreed to something unheard-of with the brothers, but she had no interest in Mr. Smith. No matter how badly she wanted to make things right for her grandfather, she could never fuck the nasty old manager. Farm or no farm, she had secretly wanted Colton and Waylon in her bed.

He grabbed her wrist and pulled her behind him as he moved toward the narrow hallway. She struggled and planted her heels heavily on the floor to ground herself. "I'm not fucking you. No way in hell. If you don't wanna talk business, I'm leaving."

"Who said anything about fucking? I'll settle for you sucking my dick. I bet you'll like it." He rubbed his erection, still holding her wrist with his other hand.

"I said no!" She pulled back hard, lost her balance, and hit her head on the side of the table. Her vision blacked briefly, and her head pulsed, the sound of blood rushing through her ears.

The next events were a blur, like a dream. He was touching her, feeling her full breasts, and then heaving her dead weight onto the conference table. Half in, half out of reality, she began to struggle, moaning from the pain and what she assumed was happening. She had to get her wits to fight him off, or God knows what he'd do to her. A man like him had no honor. He'd fuck her near-lifeless body and enjoy every perverted second of it.

He tore her shirt down the middle. The sound of fabric tearing forced a rush of adrenaline into her blood. She forced open her eyes and willed all her energy into her limbs to fight off her attacker. Jack wasn't young, wasn't fit, wasn't even on the skinny side, but his one-track mind gave him impossible male strength that kept her pinned on the table.

"Stop struggling, you little bitch." He slapped her, which only helped pull her into the present, into a proper state of mind after her momentary blackout.

"Get off me!" She screamed as loud as she could with his weight pressing against her chest as he fiddled with his belt buckle.

She managed to wriggle one of her arms free and grabbed a handful of his thin, wispy hair. He roared and brought a hand to her neck. Callie twisted and turned, flailing all her limbs in the hope of making contact with his body.

"What in tarnation is going on here?" Thank God! As soon as Callie heard Colton's deep baritone voice echo in the large room, she went limp, too tired to fight a second longer. Colton may have betrayed her trust, but she still had faith in him not to harm her, to protect her, even. Jack pulled off her and adjusted his clothes. Callie lay on the table, her shirt split, exposing her pink lace bra. She was too exhausted even to care or to move.

"Nothing at all," said Jack.

"That wasn't nothing. She was fighting you off, Jack. What kind of man are you?"

Callie rose to her elbows, surveying the room, still slightly dazed. As Colton spoke, he moved steadily forward, like a brick wall, forcing Jack to back up. They didn't compare in size. Colton's shadow alone would swallow up the older man's. The secretary was also in the room now, her hands clasped over her mouth and nose in shock.

"She wanted it. Trust me."

"No. She didn't. How would you like to feel fear? Huh? Have someone stronger than you force you down and assault you?" His words came out as pointed threats. Would there be a fight? Would Colton beat the tar out of Jack Smith in defense of her honor? Just the thought sent warm tingles cascading through her.

"Colton? What's going on?" Boyd entered the office. After a quick assessment, his eyes remained fixed on Callie.

"Jack was forcing himself on Callie. Luckily, I showed up when I did, or things would have gotten a lot worse."

"He hurt you, darlin'?" Boyd used an arm to her back to help her sit straight. He started to pull her shirt closed, his fingers brushing against her nipples, but stopped and lifted off his own shirt and passed it to her. "Put this on. I'll drive you home."

"Good idea, Boyd. I'll deal with Jack. Seems you can't hire good help these days. Waylon was right—never trust a man in a cheap suit."

Boyd escorted her to the door with slow steps and gentle handling, as if she may break. The secretary followed them out of the office. Though Callie supposed she should be traumatized by her near rape, she only noticed the heat radiating off Boyd's bare flesh pressed against her side. He had a body to die for, the same as his brothers'— defined muscle, soft skin over steel, with a flawless golden sheen.

"You okay, sweetheart?" The woman brushed Callie's hair off her face with both hands once they were in the parking area and then held her cheeks in her palms to get a better look at her. "Poor thing. Don't you worry. Colton will deal with Mr. Smith."

"I'm okay now. I hit my head, or else he'd never have gotten me pinned the way he had." She was more embarrassed for being the victim when she prided herself on her strength and control.

The woman laughed. "Oh, I believe that! Colton's been telling me what a spitfire you are. The men need a woman like you around here to set them straight." She helped Boyd lead her to his truck. "Don't you fret, sweetheart. I'm sure these big boys will help straighten out all your troubles now that the fox is getting thrown out of the henhouse."

"I'm not a hen, Mary Sue." Boyd frowned as he helped Callie up into the passenger seat.

"Of course not." She gave Callie a conspiratorial wink. "You're a rooster through and through, Boyd. Now, off you go, and take good care of her."

* * * *

Boyd's day had sure taken a turn for the dramatic. He'd never expected to find Callie on their property again. At least not until he was able to resolve the land issue. When he saw Callie lying on the table, so petite and fragile, her shirt torn open, he thought he'd lose precious control. Luckily, Colton was there to deal with that asshole, Jack. The manager better not show his face around the Black Corporation again, or it'd be the worst mistake of his life, next to laying a finger on Callie.

Knowing another man had touched her, especially against her will, brought out the beast within the man. He hadn't thought twice about tugging off his own shirt to cover her. Nobody should be looking at her half-dressed…except him. Boyd hadn't stopped thinking about Callie since the day he'd dropped her off at her farmhouse. Day and night, he sported a hard-on for her. Having her in his arms, fragile and lacking her usual irritation, felt like heaven, and he realized he was more lost to the female than he'd first thought.

As they neared Callie's farm, she laid a hand on his forearm. "I can't go home like this. My grandpa will know something's wrong. I don't want him upset." Boyd slowed the truck down. "Can you take me into town?"

"Sure." The perfect opportunity had presented itself, and Boyd wasn't going to let the chance slip away. "How about I buy you lunch at the diner? When you're ready, I'll drive you back home."

She smiled and gave him a slight nod. The woman had the most beautiful smile, the kind that made men stop in their tracks just to stare. He'd never seen it on her before and wanted to see it again and again.

Things would be different between them now. With Jack gone, he knew he'd be able to find a settlement for the land issue that would leave everyone happy. As soon as he got home, he'd go through Jack's files and acquaint himself better with the restructuring plan. If he had taken charge in the beginning, they'd never be in this mess. Hiring outsiders to help run a family business was damn foolish and lazy.

Callie remained quiet for the drive, looking out the passenger-side window. No doubt she was still shook up from Jack's manhandling. His need to make things right for her surprised him. He cared what she thought of him, and he wanted her happy.

As they pulled in front of the diner, Boyd realized being shirtless would be a problem. No shirt, no service, and the restaurant owners held fast to their rules with so many unruly cowboys visiting the town.

"Mind if we take a walk before we eat? I'm in need of a shirt." He winked as he helped her out of the cab.

"You should take yours back." She started to slip the shirt up, but he stilled her hands.

"It's yours. Don't you worry. There're a couple shops up the way where I can pick up a new one."

They walked along the sidewalk of the sleepy country town. The few men who passed them took time taking Callie in head to toe. His glare of ownership kept them moving along their way. Being in Callie's presence felt natural, felt comfortable, even though he barely knew her. She wasn't a buckle bunny or more concerned with her hair and makeup than him. A natural, down-to-earth beauty. When he reached for her hand, he expected her to pull away as she had in the past, but she surprised him and entwined her fingers with his. She even rewarded him with another little smile as she looked up to meet his eyes.

* * * *

Callie knew Boyd was different from his brothers from day one. The time he drove her home from his ranch only proved her belief. He tried to help her, and his genuine, old-fashioned manners pulled her toward him like an invisible force. Walking beside Boyd, all bare-chested and damn tempting, she thought she'd faint when he reached for her hand. The warm, calloused surface of his strong hand melted the frigid barrier around her. Boyd was all right. She wouldn't try and fight her feelings for him as she did with Colton and Waylon, who were clearly no good for her.

Callie wondered if Boyd had the same sexual appetite as his brothers. She could only hope. Having a strong, virile cowboy for a boyfriend was something Callie had always dreamed of. With her libido at soaring heights, much worse after her time with the Black brothers, she needed a real man, one who could satisfy her. Though she tried to focus all her energy on the man beside her, she couldn't keep her mind from continually drifting to those two womanizers. She hated them and wanted them in equal parts.

They entered a men's clothing store. Boyd didn't fancy-foot around. He marched over to a rack, glanced briefly at the items, measuring size by giving the material a stretch, then pulled two shirts free from their hangers.

"That all for you, Boyd?" asked the portly man behind the counter.

"That's all. As you can see, I'm in dire need of shirts." He chuckled and pulled out his black leather wallet. Callie leaned against the wall at the end of the counter, gazing appreciatively at the muscles moving in Boyd's sides and shoulders as he handed the man some bills.

"Who's your friend?"

Boyd cleared his throat and looked over at her. She was curious to see how he'd introduce her. "This is Callie. We have some business dealings."

Callie frowned. Business dealings? She wanted much more from Boyd, especially now that she expected the problems with her farm to clear up. At least, she hoped Mary Sue had been right and everything would get settled now that Jack was gone. What did she expect Boyd to say? They hadn't had a first date, never mind not being intimate. If she wanted more from Boyd, she'd have to make her intentions crystal clear to the cowboy before she lost her chance. Once the business end of things cleared up, she had her horses, and the farm was safe, he'd be out of her life for good. Her only hope at a happily ever after would be Josh Evans, and she'd rather die an old spinster than give him the time of day.

"Business? Ain't that the shirt I sold you last month?" The man nodded to Callie's attire. Boyd's shirt hung to her thighs.

"Now, that ain't any business of yours, Phil. Mind your manners around a lady."

"Of course." He passed a bag and receipt to Boyd over the counter with a wink and said his good-byes.

Once outside, back in the warm sunshine, he asked Callie to hold the bag while he slipped on one of the shirts, a dark navy T-shirt that hugged his broad shoulders and defined chest deliciously. She was sad to see him cover up, but he looked good clothed and naked. How would the rest of him fare? Judging by the large size of his cowboy boots and rough, man-sized hands, he'd be well endowed. Just the thought sent blood rushing to her pussy, making it throb and ache for what he could no doubt deliver.

Before they could make it to the diner, someone called out from a table in front of a coffee shop. She assessed the two old men and realized one was her grandfather. Out of bed and in town.

"Grandpa? What are you doing out here?" He sat with one of his best friends. She had to admit, her grandpa looked happy, even sun kissed, and healthier than he had been in awhile. Still, she didn't approve of him being out and about without even a mention.

"You took off like a bat out of hell this morning before I could tell you Al was picking me up."

"You should be resting."

"Nonsense. But you should call Josh. I have a heavy load of potatoes that I need transferred into Al's truck before he drives me home. Too heavy for you, Callie."

No way was she calling Josh. Before she could argue that she was more than capable of hauling potatoes on her own, Boyd chimed in. "I wouldn't mind helping, sir. Where is your load at?"

"What a fine young man. Aren't you going to introduce your friend?"

"Of course. This is Boyd Black. He lives a few farms over."

Her grandfather set his coffee cup on the round glass table and sat straighter with sudden interest. "A Black boy? You're Bobby's son?"

"Yes, sir."

"A good man, your father."

"Thank you, sir."

The conversation was short, and they were soon on their way to pick up the potatoes. Callie followed along behind Boyd as he balanced a large burlap sack on each shoulder with ease. She liked that he spoke respectfully to her kin, and her grandpa seemed to like him in return. If she brought Boyd home as a potential husband, her grandpa would probably give her his blessing. Of course, marriage planning was a tad premature considering they hadn't even made it to the diner for their first unofficial date.

Dropping the sacks in the back of his own pickup with a loud echo, he sat on the tailgate, brushing his hands through his thick chocolate-brown hair. "There." He exhaled, and a mischievous glint appeared in his eyes. "Come here."

Callie approached him cautiously. He didn't scare her, and she'd have been lying if she'd said she didn't want him, but she cared what he thought of her. She wasn't the whore his brothers thought she was.

Boyd hooked an arm around her waist and pulled her forward. She ended up standing with one of his jean-clad thighs between her legs, unmercifully pressing against her swollen clit. "Why are you afraid of me?"

"I never said I was." Being so close to him, and being able to smell his rich, masculine scent, sent warmth coursing through her.

"But you are. I feel you pulling away when I'm trying to inch closer." She felt his fingers biting into her side, not painfully, but insistent.

"How can I pull away? You've done nothing to court me. Do you expect me to hop into bed with you for carrying the potatoes? Because I could have managed myself, always have."

"There you go, getting all defensive again." He was right. Every muscle in her body had gone stiff. She always expected the worst from people. It saved her from the constant disappointment she'd become accustomed to early on in life.

Giving in to Colton and Waylon Black had been simple enough. She'd done it for her grandfather. It had nothing to do with emotions or a future. Anything she decided to do with Boyd would be real, and she could get hurt. But the man was irresistible. His dark lashes framed brilliant blue eyes. He scrubbed his jawline, thick with stubble, before reaching out and running a finger over her cheek. He whispered, "I'm not going to hurt you, Callie." She melted at his comforting words, dropping heavily over his leg, heightening her arousal.

Filthy images filtered through her head. She wouldn't stop him if he flipped her around and fucked her in the truck bed. Her need pressed so deep, she didn't even care if they had an audience. *Kiss me, dammit!*

"We better head off to the diner before it gets too late." He released her, and as he slipped off the tailgate, she felt the loss of his body pressing tightly against her own. She didn't want to eat. She wanted Boyd, hopefully for keeps.

Chapter Eleven

Boyd was finding it difficult to be a gentleman with Callie. She deserved to be courted properly, but his cock ached in his jeans, hard as steel. When she sat on his leg like a young girl riding a pony, he could swear he felt the heat from her pussy searing into him. She supported herself by gripping his shoulders, testing out his muscles with her slender fingers. He wanted her gripping him during sex. Hell, she could scratch and bite him if she wanted, he wouldn't complain.

Resisting her and suggesting they head to the diner took every last ounce of his resolve. Then his cell phone rang, giving him a much-needed distraction from the blonde temptation.

"Boyd, where you at?"

"Heading to the diner in town. With Callie."

Colton remained silent for a moment. "I thought you were taking her home."

"She wasn't ready to head home, so I'm taking her out. Don't be bothering me now."

"Hey! We found her horses at a boarding farm. You're gonna have to go through some of these papers, too. They're confusing the hell out of me and Waylon."

"Yeah. Sure. Tomorrow." Boyd snapped his cell phone shut, turned it off, and took Callie's hand in his for the walk to the diner.

After choosing a booth, they slipped in opposite sides to face each other. The worn, red vinyl seats were cracked and the linoleum on the table stained. He wished this wasn't the best place to eat in town because Callie deserved better. Boyd had money he rarely enjoyed, but he'd love to spend some on Callie, make her feel like the princess she was. Hell, he wanted to claim her as his and make the world go away. No more worries, no more bills. He wanted to be everything she needed.

* * * *

"Boyd. Good to see you in here. It's been awhile." The waitress had a blonde bob and was so heavy on the makeup, Callie bet her face would crack if she smiled. She had a cute figure, though, and the way she spoke to Boyd said they knew each other well. An odd sense of jealousy burned in her gut, clawing its way out, but she kept a mask of disinterest on her face.

"How're things, Sharon?"

"Good and lonely."

Callie ground her molars together to keep from saying something she'd regret. She was known to speak her mind and regret it later.

They gave their orders to the woman, and as soon as she left, Boyd reached both arms across the table and beckoned for her hands. Tentatively, she offered them.

"Who was that?"

He had honest confusion written on his face for a moment, having already forgotten about the waitress. "Oh, that's Waylon's girlfriend, Sharon."

Somehow, the news didn't make her feel much better. Knowing Waylon had a girlfriend made Callie feel more the whore than she already felt. Boyd was still safely on the market and ripe for her picking, but knowing Waylon was taken filled her with gloom. Why? Colton and Waylon only wanted their way with her sexually. Though the morning had been one of the most amazing experiences of her life and Waylon was a master of seduction, he was a player. The man had a girlfriend but had still partaken in shoving a plastic dick up Callie's ass while sucking her pussy. How would Sharon feel about learning such news? Still, a part of her wanted him to want her more than he wanted Sharon. Which was ridiculous.

"He has a girlfriend? You sure about that?"

"Well, she's been his flavor for the past couple months. That says a lot about her."

"And Colton, does he have a *flavor*?"

"Every flavor under the sun…but he never keeps them." He pulled her hands closer, forcing her to lean over the table. "You haven't asked about me, Callie."

"I just assumed you were available. If you had a girlfriend, I'd think she'd mind you taking me out to lunch."

"And what about you? Do you belong to another man? It's hard to believe a beauty like you is unattached."

"Well, believe it. And I would never belong to anyone. If I had a man, he'd belong to me."

He leaned over the table to join her in the middle. Intensity shone in his eyes. Then the brush of his lips against hers just before whispering, "Can I be your man?"

She couldn't help but smile against his lips, even though all she wanted was to kiss him. "Do I get a test drive?"

"You're being naughty, Callie. Good girls don't talk like that." He licked the seam of her lips, his breath heavy.

"Then I guess you don't want a sample." She pulled back, half insulted, half playful. He sat properly in his seat, his hand disappearing under the table, no doubt to adjust his cock. She loved that she could affect him, affect men as a whole.

"Give me a sample, Callie. Don't be cruel."

She peered around the inside of the diner. There were a few people sitting on stools at the counter, and two other booths were filled. Then she spotted the sign for the restrooms. "Meet me in the ladies' room." She wet her lips for emphasis and slipped out of the booth.

* * * *

"Fucking slow down!" shouted Waylon, holding on to the dashboard. Gravel sprayed and dust clouded around their truck as Colton navigated the back roads at well above the speed limit.

"I bet you he's fucking her this minute. She should be ours after all the work we put in."

"What work? We lied to her, took advantage of her." Waylon saw the determination in his brother's face. He'd never seen him like this. Not for a piece of ass. There was no doubt in Waylon's mind that Colton had feelings for Callie. He knew his brother too well for him to disguise it. Now he wanted to have a showdown with Boyd over a woman who belonged to neither of them. It couldn't end up well.

"Things are different now. I can promise her the farm and mean it."

"Too late for that. You've already showed your true colors."

Colton's head snapped to the side like an enraged bull. "What colors? What are you saying, little brother?"

"I'm saying you're acting crazy over a piece of tail. It's not like you. The only reason you want her now is because Boyd's moving in on her. It's always a competition between you two."

"And who always wins?"

Waylon shook his head and continued to focus on the perilous ride. Colton could pretend all he wanted, but Waylon knew better.

They came to an abrupt halt in the parking lot of the diner. Colton flew out the driver's door before Waylon even got his belt off.

* * * *

Boyd waited a couple of minutes after Callie went to the bathroom before he joined her. He didn't want to arouse any suspicion amongst the diner patrons. Those minutes felt like an eternity when she made such sweet promises.

He pushed open the bathroom door at the end of the dim corridor and found her sitting on the counter, kicking her legs like a child. He turned and flipped the door lock.

"Where's my sample, darlin'?"

"What happens after I give it to you? Do I ever see you again?" There was genuine conflict in her big doe eyes. She'd been through enough heartache trying to save her farm. He didn't want to add to it. Didn't plan on adding to it.

"That's what a sample's all about. Once you get a taste, you have to have more."

Another precious smile. He rushed over, took his place between her thighs, and cupped her ass to pull her to the edge. When her mound slammed into his rigid cock, he let out a groan.

"Kiss me," she said. Her voice was seductive, a breathy whisper. She wrapped her arms around his neck and secured him against her body with her legs around his hips.

Boyd dropped his head and nuzzled her neck, trailing his tongue along the erogenous zone behind her ear. She shuddered in response and ground her pussy into his erection.

"Please. Kiss me, Boyd."

He couldn't deny her, not when he wanted to taste those pretty pink lips for himself. With all the control he could muster, he kissed her. Soft at first, absorbing her texture and taste, then more intensely, invading her mouth with his tongue.

Forget the sampling, he wanted it all. He began to unbuckle his belt while trying to fight her greedy little hands searching for his cock. Damn, he wanted to give it to her in more ways than one. Seeing their passion unfold from firsthand view and the image reflected in the mirrored wall behind the sinks made the act more spectacular. He'd like to take her someplace other than a filthy public washroom, but they were beyond rational thought now.

He moaned when she pulled his cock free. She circled the length with a fist, squeezing and testing. Her satisfied smirk made him ever harder, if that were possible.

"I want to taste you, Boyd."

She knew exactly what to say. Such a sweet thing with a wicked mouth was an irresistible combination.

"Whatever you want, darlin'." She pushed him back by the chest and slipped off the counter. Dropping to her knees, she parted her lips and gripped his cock.

The pounding on the door began just before her swollen lips could taste his head. He wanted to tell her to ignore the disruption and continue, but the bastard wouldn't stop banging.

"Open the door, Boyd! Sharon said you're in there with Callie."

"Fuck," Boyd muttered as he rearranged himself and zipped up. He pulled Callie to her feet, kissed her forehead, and then opened the door.

Colton burst in, slamming the door into the wall behind it with a hollow bang, looking about like a madman.

"What the hell is your problem?" Boyd asked, putting himself in front of Callie.

His older brother looked as if he were at a loss for words, opening his mouth to speak but shutting it instead.

"Why do you have Callie holed up in the ladies' room? Explain that to me, Boyd."

Callie spoke for him. "Why do you care? I'm not your concern or your property. In fact, I was planning to fuck your brother good and proper since you obviously couldn't finish the job."

Colton's face reddened with anger or embarrassment or a mixture of both. He wasn't used to back-talking women.

"Why Boyd? What's wrong with me or Waylon?"

"He didn't lie to me! He didn't try to use me like some cheap whore when I was at my most vulnerable. He's been nothing but a perfect gentleman. You should both learn from him."

"I told you it wasn't like it seemed. Come, let me get you out of here. If you think this is the place a gentleman takes a lady, I have a lot to show you."

He grabbed Callie's upper arm and began to drag her out of the small washroom.

"Oh, no!" Boyd stepped in the way, pushing his brother off his step, making him stumble slightly. "She's mine and ain't going anywhere with you." Boyd had had no idea that there was a history between Callie and his brothers, but it didn't matter. He wasn't about to let them steal her away as they did with countless of his girlfriends growing up.

Before a fight could break out, Callie spoke up. She pressed a hand to both their chests while addressing the three of them. "Look, Colton...Waylon, I don't know why either of you are here. You don't own me, and since Jack's gone, you can't buy me."

"You were ready to sell yourself this morning," said Colton. "Maybe I still plan on taking over your farm. Maybe you should show me how much you want it." His eyes were hooded as he bent over into Callie's space. Did she cast the same spell over all men?

"That's enough!" Boyd demanded. He wouldn't allow his brother to threaten and extort an innocent woman for sex. That was wrong on so many levels. Why was he the only one to see that? Of course, Waylon always went along with Colton's antics without a word of protest.

Chapter Twelve

Callie felt pissed off with all these big, strong cowboys making a play for her. She wasn't some disposable toy for their amusement. Still, as much as she wanted to push past them and get out of their lives forever, she couldn't. The testosterone felt heavy in the room. She could smell leather, musky cologne, and horses mixed with that distinct maleness in the small space. All three men towered over her, broad shouldered and fit from working the land. Being as petite as she was, she knew they wouldn't hurt her. Not physically, but her emotions were another story entirely.

Even though Mary Sue and Boyd had said all would be well with her farm, she wouldn't be happy until she had it in black and white that the state no longer had interest in her property. She needed her taxes lowered to the standard rate of her neighbors' and the phone calls and eviction notices to stop. Until she knew her grandpa's legacy was safe, she couldn't cold-shoulder the brothers too much. Did she even want to?

"It's okay, Boyd. I can handle Colton."

"I'd like to see you try, sweet thing." Colton smirked and tugged her chin up to look at him. "Ready for some more games?"

Callie's pussy throbbed at the mention of games. She remembered being bound by rope and tortured with rough hands and searing kisses. She wondered what other toys Waylon carried in his saddlebags. Wondered and wanted to find out. She had enjoyed being the submissive, letting them take control of her body, knowing exactly how to pleasure her. They may have played her for a fool last time, but she'd be smarter this time and get them to sign something.

Callie trusted Boyd. If he witnessed a deal for her farm, she imagined they'd be forced to keep their word or face off with him.

It would be nice to have Colton look at her with the longing desire associated with true love, not just lust. Same with Waylon, the man with a girlfriend in the next room. But if she had Boyd, she'd be a very happy woman. Forget about living alone as a spinster with twenty barn cats. She had a chance at real, long-term happiness. If she gave in to Colton's wishes, would Boyd want nothing to do with her? What should she risk? The farm or the love of a good man?

"What kind of games?" She played the innocent, trying to gauge her situation and Boyd's reactions.

Colton tucked loose hair behind her ears. "We could start where we left off—you naked and tied to the ground, your sweet pussy hungry and inviting. I'll fuck you with my tongue until you're begging me to make you come."

"Crude, Colton. Fucking crude," said Boyd, pulling her back.

"Don't tell me you don't want her. You may have never wanted to play our games before, but you damn sure want her. Maybe it's time to join your brothers in a little fun."

"That'll be the day," he muttered.

The image of all three Black brothers sharing her, pleasuring her, making love to her, was one she couldn't get out of her head. With the seed planted, she realized she wanted nothing more. She could enjoy Colton and Waylon's games and powerful sexuality while enjoying the man she hoped would want her for more than just cheap thrills. Would she ever be able to convince Boyd to engage in one wicked ménage with her and his brothers?

"Maybe it wouldn't be so bad. I mean, you're brothers, you should be used to sharing things," she almost whispered, afraid of his reaction.

"Not women. Not me, anyway. Is that what you want, Callie?" The look of hurt and disappointment that flushed his handsome face made her lust fizzle away.

"Of course not." She shook her head from the cloud of male heat threatening to engulf her. Her logic was buried in the haze, and she needed to snap out of it and return to the responsible woman she'd always been. No fucking around in public washrooms with men whom she wouldn't see the next day.

"Good. Then don't listen to these fools. Nobody is going to ask you to trade your body for your property. We'll work this all out tomorrow, but it'll be fine. I promise." Boyd accentuated his final words, looking at Colton when he said them.

They returned to their booth, and much to Boyd's chagrin, his brothers took the next booth behind him. She couldn't help but giggle when they made faces behind their serious brother's back. Refocusing, she met Boyd's hard gaze.

"I like you, Callie. You're just the kind of cowgirl I need in my life."

"Really?" This was what she wanted, wasn't it? She'd always cringed at the thought of settling down with a boring man like Josh. Boyd wasn't boring, but raw male sexuality in a tight pair of Wranglers. She needed to know more about him, though, about the man within, before she committed. Callie played for keeps. Once she decided to give a man her heart, she'd be in for the long haul, ups and downs and all. While the thought of a life with Boyd thrilled her and filled her with the warmth of belonging, she couldn't ignore the draw his two brothers continued to have over her. For some reason, she saw the three of them as a whole, good and bad all swirled into one perfect union—foolish thoughts that were liable to get her into a heap of trouble.

"Of course, darlin'. Can't you see the way you affect me?" He leaned over the table and whispered to keep their conversation private from his eavesdropping brothers. "I can see a future for us. I love my family to death, even my fool brothers, but a part of me, deep inside, always felt like an outsider."

"Why would you say that?"

"Not many people know that I was adopted before Waylon was born. I can't remember a time anyone pointed out that I wasn't blood, but I still feel it here." He pressed his hand over his heart, his eyes sincere and focused on her.

Just that brief glimpse into the man behind the beautiful exterior warmed her heart. She felt connected to him on a deeper, more intimate level because she knew his plight too well. Callie knew how it felt to be an outsider, to not feel like you belonged even though those around you showered you with love.

"I wasn't adopted. Well, I suppose I was, in a way. My mother gave me up when I was born, and I never knew my daddy. Guess that's why it's so important for me to save my grandpa's farm. He raised me, did everything to make me happy in life."

"You're a complicated woman, Callie." He reached for her hand and kissed her knuckles. "Let's get out of here."

Just before they slipped out of the booth, Sharon sidled up to the next booth and wrapped her arms around Waylon, who faced her. Why did he stare at her while his girlfriend vied for his attention? Why did Colton turn around to gauge her reaction? Did they feel her irrational jealousy surging out of her in violent waves? Did they sense that she wanted to jump up and fling the clingy bitch off her man?

Callie shifted her gaze from Waylon's to Boyd's, seeking an anchor for her traitorous emotions that seemed unbridled as of late. Why did she feel such ownership over the Black brothers? She supposed the wickedly delicious things they did to her body could be blamed.

Boyd attempted to lead her out of the diner with a hand to the small of her back, which snapped her out of her reverie. She bolted to a standstill for a moment, tempted to tell Waylon to come pick up the dildo he left at her ranch, but it wasn't her place to upset Boyd or Sharon because of her jealousy. Grinding her molars and giving both Colton and Waylon a glare of pure malice, she allowed Boyd to lead her to his truck.

"Should we pick up your grandfather?"

"Are you kidding? He'd skin me for embarrassing him in front of his friend. He'll get a drive home from whoever brought him into town." Boyd held the door open for her, and she climbed up onto the bench. Besides the issues she had with the other two men, she felt surprisingly content. The mess with the farm that had plagued her for months, years, even, was finally going to end. A wash of peace created by saving her grandfather's farm and finding the affections of a good man made her dizzy. As soon as she had Paddy back, she'd be right as rain.

The drive down the long driveway felt like the green mile, the longest couple of minutes in Callie's life. She didn't want to say good-bye to Boyd, even for the day. It wasn't just the coiled sexual tension stored in her body from all the torturous stimulation throughout the day, but more. She wanted to bond with the man she planned on giving her heart to. Boyd Black, the adopted son of a million-dollar cattleman. One with feelings, dreams, desires—and she couldn't forget the face and body to die for.

Callie watched as Boyd effortlessly flung the sacks of potatoes over his shoulders and carried them to her shed. The hour was growing late, a faint chill blowing in with the setting sun. As soon as she opened the metal doors to the storage shed, the dogs got loose, circling the man they'd never met. She forgot she hadn't set them loose to protect the property when she left. The shed was huge and retrofitted to store goods and house the dogs during inclement weather.

The typical growling and snarling ensued. To her surprise, Boyd didn't appear shaken, but continued into the shed and dropped the sacks in a dark corner, only to return to the entrance. He leaned against the frame, arms crossed, eyeing the dogs with a slight smirk.

"They love you," he said.

"I know." She looked at the bared fangs of her three dogs and smiled. "These are three males I can count on to love me to the death."

He ran a hand through his thick brown hair, the shadows of the evening highlighting the sharp masculine lines of his face.

"That's enough!" ordered Callie, clapping her hands once. It was all the command needed for the dogs to visibly relax. Like her horses, her dogs were well trained, and she was proud of her tutelage. "Do you want to come in for a minute?"

The house was empty, and the idea of being alone with Boyd after what they'd almost done in the restroom sent jitters of excitement racing up her spine. He seemed so mellow, so in control. She wanted him to lose his head and make love to her with enough passion to rock the little old house.

"Sure." He followed her to the front porch, the dogs sniffing him curiously as he moved.

Upon entering the modest house, Boyd separated from her, strolling around to take in the interior. He looked at the many pictures on the walls of Callie growing up and of her grandmother, who had passed away several years earlier. Bending over, he blew the dust off the brass nameplates from the many trophies on the wooden shelf, reading the titles aloud before turning to her.

"You must be quite the horseman…or horsewoman." He stretched up to his full height, looking too big, too masculine, to be standing in her living room.

"I could probably show you a trick or two."

He continued to look around the small room filled with out-of-date furniture and nothing in the way of luxury. "So just the two of you live here?"

"Yep. Just us, now that my grandma is gone. Must be nothing like your place. I could just imagine."

He snagged her hand, pulling her to sit beside him on the worn fabric sofa. "You have the wrong idea in your head, Callie. It's just me and my brothers most of the year, and they're rarely home. We live simply. Very simply." His tone alone told stories filled with sleepless nights and lonesome days.

"You sound almost as lonely as me." She couldn't help but caress his cheek, the stubble tickling her fingertips.

"It's about time I settled down with the right woman." Boyd licked his lips and leaned closer, his eyes heavy, lust-drunk, and lips so tempting. Callie suddenly noticed how quiet the house was as twilight settled in, shading the room, creating an intimacy on its own. Boyd brushed his lips to hers and then cupped her face to deepen the kiss.

She twisted her hips so she could move in closer. Running her hands up his chest, she finally settled her arms around his neck. He kissed well, his lips thick and sensual, his tongue lively and explorative. When she started to feel his low groans vibrating up from his chest, she knew he'd passed the point of no return. She dropped one hand and tugged at his thick leather belt.

"You sure about this?" he asked, only releasing his mouth to ask the question.

"Don't you want me?"

"Oh, God, Callie. Don't even ask me that. I want you so much it hurts. I just don't want you to think I'm after one thing, like my brothers."

"I know you're different." She pulled away from him and lifted her shirt off over her head. His eyes flashed to her generous cleavage. "Show me how a real cowboy makes love, Boyd."

Chapter Thirteen

He knocked her to her back as he hovered over her, suddenly urgent. The feel of his heat and weight suspended over her made her pussy cream and heart beat to an erratic beat. She unbuckled his leather belt in the confined space between their bodies. The task was more difficult with him trying to unbutton her jeans and slip his hand past the edge of her panties. She arched to help him, becoming more and more desperate to get naked and have him inside her.

"I can't wait," she muttered. Forget about making love slow and sweet. Not today, not the first time. If they were both true to each other, there would be more days for patient exploration.

Boyd stood and hooked his fingers into her pants at her sides and yanked down, bringing her legs and hips high in the air as he removed her clothes. The panties came off easily, and he shuddered when he saw her exposed sex. Before joining her on the sofa, he kicked off his own jeans and tugged off his new shirt. He was about to lose his boxer briefs when she bolted upright.

"Not here. My grandpa sits here to watch TV. Take me to my room." She didn't mean to literally take her, but he did, scooping her up easily into his arms. Callie navigated the way to her bedroom, and he kicked the door shut after they entered. Even though she was nearly naked, her cheeks flushed when she saw his expression upon seeing her room for the first time.

An array of pinks and pastels, rows of teddy bears, and porcelain dolls along the dressers and shelves. It was a monument to her childhood. She supposed she should have redecorated years ago, but it had never entered her mind until now. Most days, she was busy with the farm and only came to her room late at night to crash.

He laid her on her bed over the lace-trimmed, pink comforter. "I don't know if I can perform with so many eyes watching me." He chuckled as he scanned the inhuman audience.

"I have faith in you." Callie unclipped and wiggled out of her bra, leaving herself completely nude. She never thought of her body as a sexual object, more a workhorse, but the way Boyd devoured her figure made her overly self aware. Her body prepared itself for his invasion, and moisture trickled toward her anus, clit swollen and throbbing. One touch and she might explode.

She'd already seen his cock at the diner, and she eagerly wanted to make its acquaintance again. As if reading her thoughts, he pushed the offending material down his legs, revealing a thick, monstrous cock. It pointed slightly upwards, and from her angle, she could see the prominent vein pulsing along the length of his shaft. Callie needed to feel it, test if it was as hard as it appeared.

"I've wanted you since the first day I saw you." He crawled over her, his muscular arms tensing as he supported his weight above her. Besides playtime with his brothers, it had been eons since she'd had a man. Those boys from her memories had barely passed puberty, didn't know what they were doing, did not have bodies like her Black brothers, and she had been too young and inexperienced to enjoy herself. Tonight was different in every way. She was a woman, with a real man...a cowboy, no less. He'd be able to show her what sex was meant to be like, and her anticipation made it difficult to catch her breath.

"I recall screaming down your neck that first day." She shuddered as his hot breath tickled her neck. He only ran his lips over her skin, not kissing or tasting, just that gentle brush, which ignited all her hidden desires.

"Didn't matter." He inhaled her scent, and she couldn't stop from arching her pelvis up, so desperate for his heat, his cock. "You were adorable. I don't quite remember what you said, but I couldn't keep my eyes off your body."

"Well, now you have me."

"I do." He parted her legs with his thigh and rested against her aching mound. His cock was harder than anything natural should feel and rubbed her sensitive nub in a torturous rhythm. The man knew how to move his body, how to tease and tempt.

She wanted to scream at him to fuck her already. Touch her, taste her, anything, but no more sweet agony.

When she heard a crinkling sound by her ear, she twisted her head to look. Boyd had a single condom wrapper pressed between two fingers.

"How did you get that in here with no clothes on?"

His resulting playful smirk made her desperate to eat him alive. "There's a lot about me you don't know, darlin'."

He stared at her, and with only the remnants of daylight peeking through the curtains, his eyes took on a deep ocean blue. Biting the corner of his bottom lip as if thinking of the right words to say, he used one hand to smooth back her hair, his eyes filled with adoration for her. Could it be possible? Could all her fairy-tale dreams actually come true?

"You're beautiful. I love everything about you, right down to your little pixie nose." He leaned down and kissed the tip of her nose.

"When my grandma was alive, she told me never to believe a man that tells you sweet nothings or makes enticing promises within the first month of meeting him."

"That may be true for young men looking for a roll in the hay. I've had my fun. Now I want it all. The girl, the family, the future together."

Boyd said exactly what she needed to hear, had been waiting to hear all her adult life. But happily ever after wasn't meant for her, was it? She had impure thoughts for his brothers. How could she start a relationship with a man when she craved his brothers as much as him? "What if I'm not the woman you think I am?"

He ignored her, stopping their conversation with a passion-filled kiss. Her building tension eased, and she melted into the mattress, absorbing his taste and texture with all her senses.

She pulled back to catch her breath. Her body thrummed with erotic energy, waiting to burst. Boyd crept lower, tugging her nipple into his mouth. The heat and moisture and gentle suckling made her gasp and tangle her fingers into his thick hair. With her eyes closed, she was loosening up, giving in to the numerous sensations racking her body. He trailed kisses lower, over her flat stomach, edging closer to her burning core. When low enough, he pulled up to his knees and then kneaded her breasts with both hands while kissing the quivering insides of her thighs. So many new pleasure centers came to life that she questioned if she could handle the onslaught.

"You're exactly what I want, Callie. We need each other, you and me." More kisses to her inner thighs, moving ever so slowly toward her pussy. "God, I love your tits." He gave her mounds a firm squeeze, the flesh overflowing in his clutch. "And this pretty pussy." Then he kissed her clit. The single act made her yelp, her body stirring to life in a tidal wave of ecstasy. She felt an orgasm creep rapidly to the surface, but she also wanted the night to go on forever.

"I want you inside me, Boyd. Put on the condom." When his firm lips sucked her swollen bud into his mouth, she gasped. "Please!"

"Not yet, darlin'. There ain't nothing I want more than to fuck you right now, but that's not my style. A real man has control and holds back until his lady's had at least one good climax. Trust me, it'll be better this way." He released her breasts and spread her legs wide before dropping down to his stomach. A firm lick from her anus to her clit had her shouting for more. Boyd delivered, fucking her with his tongue, sucking her pussy and teasing her clit.

"More!" she begged.

"You taste like a country woman, sweet as a ripe peach. I could eat you all day and night."

Callie pumped her hips up, needing Boyd to help her reach her climax that began to drive away her sanity. It was so close but wouldn't come.

He delivered, pulling her clit into the suction of his mouth and holding her legs down and open so she couldn't move.

"Oh, my God, I'm so close. Don't stop. Please, don't stop."

She focused on the runaway train barreling from her core outwards. It traveled in a blinding wash of ecstasy, blocking out sounds and sights and giving Callie the most incredible high of her life. Never being a good, quiet girl, she screamed with her release. She screamed for mercy, screamed Boyd's name and thanked God for the gift her lover had just given her.

Not even recovered from the intense orgasm, she heard the familiar crinkling noise. Peeking open her heavy eyelids, she watched with awe as Boyd slid the sheath over his impossibly thick dick. Even after having her release, she felt the need to suck his manly flesh and have him ravage her sensitive pussy. She may have complained about living in a man's world, but women could have multiple orgasms, and right now, she was thankful for it.

She leaned up on her elbows and smiled after he winked at her.

"Ready for more?" he asked, his voice deep and gravely.

There was no need to answer. Her reaching arms and open legs should be invitation enough. She needed to feel his naked warmth and flesh pressed against hers. All those rippling muscles of restrained male power made her ache to be filled by him.

Boyd crept up her body and positioned his cock at her entrance. He teased her, only prodding her with the mushroom head and going no farther. When she attempted to arch up to capture his length, he moved quickly, stilling her with a flat palm to the stomach.

"I knew you'd be pushy in bed," he taunted.

"I'm not pushy, you're cruel. Don't you want to feel my cunt milking your cock?"

He growled. She noticed a tick in his jaw before he plunged into her liquid center in one powerful thrust. The pressure of him filling her, stretching her like never before, made her tingle all the way to her toes. She quickly wrapped her legs around his lean waist to keep him in place. But he wasn't going anywhere. Rather, he slid a hand under the small of her back and worked her body like a finely tuned machine, pistoning in and out of her pussy with an intensity to make any woman beg to be his sex slave. Callie wanted to be his, now and forever. Just imagining days with the love of a man and nights when the beast came out to fuck made her spiral toward her next orgasm.

"Come on, darlin'," he said between pants. "Come for me before I can't hold on any longer."

She closed her eyes and focused on the feel of his dick sliding in and out, fast and deep, his coarse pubic hair crushing against her swollen clit with each thrust. Callie was on the cusp of the wave, ready to go over. Just a few more pumps from his hips, and she'd be gone, gone, gone.

"Boyd!" She gagged and screamed. The sound muffled as she bit the thick muscle over his shoulder. He followed her this time. His sweat-slick body pounded harder, without restraint for a few more moments, and then he collapsed over her with a satisfied groan.

Though she wanted more than anything to just fall asleep in his arms since her exhaustion was controlling her body now, she heard a truck door slam shut.

Chapter Fourteen

"And where the fuck have you been? I've been calling your cell all night."

Waylon reclined on the sofa as Boyd entered the living room of their family home. This would be a good show. Colton versus Boyd...over a woman. He never thought he'd see the day. Sure, they fought over pussy, but never because they both wanted the same woman for keeps.

"Must have left it in the truck." Boyd next to ignored Colton as he brushed past him, tossing his keys on the coffee table.

"Really. And where were you at?"

Boyd turned and smiled wickedly. "Enjoying me some double Ds and sweet, young pussy."

"You didn't!"

Boyd dropped down heavily on the sofa beside Waylon. "I know you both already had your fun with her, but that's the past. She's with me now."

"Bullshit! I ain't finished with her yet. I've only just gotten started, little brother."

Boyd stood, running a hand through his hair as he exhaled like an enraged bull preparing to strike. "Stay away from her, Colton, or I'll fuck you up."

Their eldest brother laughed with full humor. "You think you can challenge me and win? Cute." Colton turned away, heading to the kitchen, calling over his shoulder, "Keep living your fantasy because it's going to blow up in your face."

Boyd returned to the sofa and kicked off his boots. "Can you believe him?"

"I think he likes your girl."

"Yeah, right. Colton's not the settling type. He's just jealous because I'm happy."

"I don't know. He's been acting strange lately. You might have one hell of a competition on your hands. You sure she's worth it?" asked Waylon.

"That woman already has my heart. It's a done deal." Boyd grabbed the remote and turned on ESPN. "It's been a crazy night. Callie's grandfather just about caught me in the house when he returned home. But I'm telling you, every second with that woman is worth the risk."

Waylon said his goodnights and made his way to his bedroom off the back kitchen. He was happy for Boyd finding love, if that's really what it was. He'd always been the responsible one but kept on the periphery of everything, including family, as if he didn't belong. As far as Waylon was concerned, Boyd was his blood brother as much as Colton. It wasn't his fault that Boyd never wanted to play their games, or they'd be just as close.

Waylon collapsed on his bed without turning on the light. The moonlight highlighted the sharp angles of his pine dresser and footboard. Not much else filled the small room. Even as a child, he never had been one to collect items of sentimental value. He lived in his older brothers' shadows. Colton was the rodeo king, the heartbreaker, the leader. Boyd was the smart one, the man's man whom people respected and obeyed, and a constant tragedy. Who was Waylon? He had yet to discover who he really was. He felt like the shell of a man and craved something to ground him, give his life more meaning than working the farm and fucking around with Colton in the evenings.

When he'd met Callie, he'd felt his heart pitter-patter to a new beat. She could be the one to change everything in his life. But as usual, he'd become the shadow when both Colton and Boyd had showed an interest in her.

He'd had countless girlfriends over the years. Even now, he supposed he was officially with Sharon, even though she knew his true nature. Sharon, like every other woman before her, liked the idea of dating a Black. It was a status symbol, some kind of difficult-to-achieve prize to snare one of them. Sharon was not the type of girl he'd want to marry or spend more than a couple of hours with at a time. She liked to talk about fashion, hairstyles, and the hottest new clubs. In comparison, Callie was a real woman, hardworking and strong-willed, with goals and morals.

After leaving the diner with his older brother steaming and cursing, he'd come home and plowed some feed fields to clear his head. With both his kin vying for the attention of the same woman, he became invisible. Truth was, he had his own interest in Callie but wouldn't admit it. There was enough friction in the house as it was.

He supposed he should be thankful. As the youngest, not much was expected from him. He was the *miracle baby*. Waylon knew his parents and the laborers thought he was a fuckup, a womanizer only interested in good times. Yes, he was the youngest, and he did enjoy many hot one-nighters and threesomes. But there was so much more to him if anyone cared to look. For once, he'd like to take control and be recognized as a contributing, feeling adult.

There was a soft rapping on his door before the hinges whined open, letting warm light from the hall cut into the room. "You awake?" asked Colton.

"Yeah."

Colton sat on the edge of the bed. The springs groaned in protest. "I want to head over to Callie's place in the morning to return the horses. You comin'?"

Even though he didn't think it was right for Colton to play more games with Callie, he couldn't say no. "Sure."

"That's a boy." Colton patted his leg a couple times, stood, and headed back toward the door.

"Hey, Colton." His brother turned back to face him, one hand on the door frame, shadows blurring his features. "What are your intentions with that girl?"

"Why you asking me that?"

Should he get involved in his brothers' competition? He couldn't help himself. Normally, he'd keep quiet, but in this case, he just had to speak out. "I've never seen Boyd so serious about a woman. He might even love her."

Colton frowned. "Whose side you on, boy?"

"Don't call me that, okay."

This would be the first time he attempted to stand up to his eldest brother or speak back. With their parents gone, Colton sometimes felt like a second father to him. But what he was doing wasn't honorable. Boyd always had two feet planted firmly on the ground, and Callie deserved a man like him, not a player like Colton.

"What's gotten into you? If you wanna spend the day with Sharon rather than indulging in that sweet cowgirl, suit yourself. But after sunrise, I'll be gone, with or without you."

* * * *

The next day, Colton enjoyed the crisp morning air as he saddled his horse. He had Callie's two geldings tied up outside, and since Waylon hadn't made an appearance, he'd tether them to his saddle horn and lead them to Callie's place himself.

Nobody would ever be able to believe that he had genuine feelings for the girl, so he wouldn't even attempt to prove it. The truth even scared him. Visiting Callie without Waylon to be his voice made him feel vulnerable. The great Colton Black sucked when it came to real emotion. He avoided such situations like the plague. The last time he'd shed a tear was at nine years old when his saddle had slipped and he'd broken two ribs. Though his mother had coddled him, he still remembered his father's words to *take it like a man.* Since then, he'd manned up and bottled his emotions, which seemed to gain him respect in several circles. Being the eldest brother also brought a lot of responsibility that his two younger siblings would never fully understand. He had an image to maintain, and sometimes, he just wanted to shed the facade and let go.

As Colton galloped across the fields, he savored the early morning sights. The sky morphed into a pale blue, and birds began to converge on the dewy fields. He took deep breaths, filling his lungs with the scents of sweet hay and morning freshness. He wondered if Callie was still asleep in her bed. If so, what was she wearing? Did she sleep in flannel, lace, or nothing at all? He could envision her in one of his T-shirts, and more possessive feelings which made him uncomfortable in his own skin began to surface.

When the little farm came into view over the horizon, his heart began to hammer in his chest in anticipation. He slowed the horses to a trot.

The cocking of a gun forced him to abruptly halt his horse. It whinnied and stomped in protest.

"Mornin', ma'am." Colton tipped his hat. The same one his dad had given him on his eighteenth birthday.

Callie scowled and continued to aim her rifle in his direction. He had to admit the woman was stealthy, having stepped out from the shadow of an outbuilding without warning. When she noticed his cargo, she dropped her weapon, making him wince from her careless disregard. She ran to the horses with an expression of unadulterated bliss.

"You brought Paddy!"

"Paddy?"

"Never mind. Untie him." She reached up, fiddling with the leather leads attached to his saddle, dangerously close to his manhood. Pushy little thing. He hardened just from the proximity of her probing hands.

He humored her, enjoying her excitement, and tossed the leads to the side of his horse. Callie gathered the horses and led them to the barn. He followed on horseback.

"You're up early," he said once she stopped, brushing her hand over the animal's neck. He wished she'd offer the same attention to him. But once she got her horses, he became invisible. He wasn't used to women not falling all over him. Though part of him felt the sting of rejection, he liked this girl. A lot.

"I run a farm by myself, Mr. Black. My day starts before dawn and doesn't end until the sun goes down."

"It's Mr. Black now? After what we shared together and with me bringing back your horses? I thought it would be Colton."

"Look. Thanks for bringing my horses back. What more do you want?"

He hopped off the side of his horse, his boots hitting the gravel in a heavy thud. Moving in slow, steady steps, each stride accented by a distinct crunch breaking the quiet morning hush, he closed the distance between them. The way she squirmed and averted her gaze told him she was uncomfortable. Good. This little vixen needed to be brought down a few notches for her own good.

"A lot more, Ms. Johnson."

"Well, I'm not interested. And I'm very busy. If you'll excuse me, I need to give these horses a medical check. God knows what they've been through since you had them stolen from me."

"That was Jack, not me."

"Whatever. Good day, Mr. Black."

He watched her lead the horses through the open barn doors. Her blonde hair was loose, and her knit sweater hugged her body, accentuating her full breasts. He remembered how her flesh had felt in his palms, how her lips had felt around his cock, and how she'd whined when Waylon had fucked her with the dildo. Just thinking about the other morning while remaining focused on her tight ass walking away made his cock ramrod hard.

Today, he took his time. His feelings were all over the place, and he was out of his comfort zone without Waylon controlling the game. Was this even a game anymore? Why was he even here? If Boyd wanted to make an honest woman of Callie, who was he to get in the way? He loved his brother, even though they'd had their friendly competitions in the past. Still, giving up Callie wasn't possible for some reason. Just thinking about it made him possessive, anxious, and his dominant nature overrode all his logic.

Colton secured his horse and slipped into the barn unbeknownst to Callie. She was squatting down, examining the horses' legs, feeling for any abrasions. As she ran her hands up and down, she cooed to the horse as if it were a young child. He admired her—her gentle hands, her sweet and spicy personality, and her natural beauty.

He moved in closer until he leaned against the opening of the stall, and then he cleared his throat. She whipped her head around, almost toppling over. "You. Why are you still here?"

"I have some unfinished business with you. Seems to me that that last time I was here we were interrupted."

She stood. Even though she maintained her ground, he saw her throat working, her eyes wide.

"Colton…"

"Tell me you didn't like it when I kissed you, when I touched you. Tell me, and I'll leave right now. You'll never see me again."

She remained silent. He supposed that was better than screaming for him to get out of her life. "Colton. I can't. I mean, I like you, but I'm not like the girls you've been with. I can't just walk away when it's all said and done and all you can offer me is one night of pleasure."

"But Boyd's different?" He couldn't help the jealousy creeping into his tone. "You don't know me at all, Callie."

"I know your type." She refocused on the horse, casting him aside with disregard. Bending over, she lifted the horse's leg and began to clear its hoof with a pick she had in her front pocket.

"Maybe you'd have better luck with men if you had better manners. I think I should teach you some."

She snickered, standing and brushing the hair out of her face. "What are you gonna do? Spank me?"

Chapter Fifteen

Just the thought of Colton punishing her, bending her naked over his lap, made her pussy weep with need. Just like the morning when Waylon and Colton had taken control, tied her up, and performed indecent sexual acts upon her body, she craved to be dominated, mastered. The feeling of release, of complete surrender, had been liberating, and she craved that rush like a cheap drug.

But Colton Black would only break her heart. She'd no doubt want more from him. More that he wouldn't be able to offer. There was something about his masculine, dominant aura, along with his rugged good looks, that pulled her in and wouldn't let go. She should run, push him away, but she couldn't bring herself to do it.

"Cat got your tongue?" He moved in, trapping her in the stall by the side of her beloved Paddy. Somehow, knowing she wasn't giving in to Colton due to some cheap trade for her farm or horses made it more thrilling, more naughty, to give in to his sinful advance.

When she didn't answer, he took her silence as an invitation. He ducked down and scooped her up over one of his broad shoulders and reversed out of the stall. She didn't kick and scream but grabbed handfuls of his shirt at his back for fear of his dropping her.

"What's upstairs?" he asked, all business.

"Just extra feed and hay."

He managed to navigate the steep, rickety ladder with her over his shoulder. His strong hand, firmly gripping her thigh, made her heart race and delicious anticipation whirl around inside her. When they emerged up in the small hayloft, he dropped her unceremoniously on a long bale of hay. She scrambled to sit up as he took in the surroundings. Along one wall was her limited collection of tack and two western saddles that were well loved, the leather shining and waiting to be used again with Paddy. It was nothing compared to the fully equipped tack room on the Black ranch, but it was hers.

"Come here," he said after sitting on a bale opposite her. He beckoned her with one crooked finger, and his eyes narrowed wickedly. What was he thinking? The way those bedroom eyes devoured her as she followed his instruction could only mean he was thinking something sinful.

Once standing in front of him, she expected him to gently take hold of her hips and maybe sit her on his lap. She expected romance and intimacy from a man incapable of either. Instead, he yanked her down roughly until she lay over his lap, stomach down. He smacked her jean-clad ass with one strong hand.

"Oh, yeah," he said before he growled and reached around to unbutton her jeans. She didn't move or fight as he tugged her tight pants past her hips, scraping her flesh as he inched them down. Callie wanted this, wanted him. She also wanted Boyd and Waylon. Not once did she think she betrayed one by being with another. In her mind, they were one entity, her Black men. Each man was a piece that created her perfect whole—but of course, that would be too easy. In the real world, a ménage relationship would never work. Even though Colton and Waylon seemed comfortable sharing her, Boyd would never go for it. He was too possessive. But weren't all three?

She wiggled to help him unclothe her. When her jeans and panties were down to her knees, she felt the air cool the moisture collected in her folds. Her pussy throbbed in eagerness for Colton's ministration.

"Tell me you've been a bad girl, Callie."

"I'm a—I'm a bad girl."

He rubbed circles over one ass cheek with his palm, warming it and making her juices flow liberally. She ached and ground her mound into his leg.

"Good. I like honesty. Ask me to punish you."

She didn't want pain. But just the physical contact with him, even if slightly unpleasant, was better than none. If she couldn't take his kind of punishment, she'd just tell him to stop.

"Punish me. I've been a very bad girl." He tortured her with his slow petting.

Before she could even tense, he lifted his hand and landed a firm slap over her ass cheek. The sound was sharp and meaty, filling the quiet space in the loft.

"Ouch!" she hollered.

He ignored her and treated the other cheek to the same treatment, a firm slap. His free hand pinned her at her lower back.

"Ask for more," he demanded while rubbing her inflamed cheeks in slow, smooth circles.

"No!"

"Callie," he warned. "Bad girls get punished, whether they like it or not. If you behave yourself, you'll learn to enjoy my discipline, even beg for more."

"Let me up!" She wiggled to free herself as much as to stimulate her swollen clit against his Wranglers. He didn't speak but smacked her again, two spanks for each cheek. Her flesh burned and throbbed but felt oddly erotic. Her core pulsed and ached for his cock. The pain mixed with her need sent her to a new plane of sensation.

He petted her tender flesh, parting her legs slightly when he reached down to her swollen folds. Dipping his fingers into her pussy, he dragged the moisture upwards in a slow sweep over her puckered anus. He followed the titillating touch with another smack.

"More!" she screamed. Callie had never intended to ask for more punishment, but the words flowed from her mouth. His resulting chuckle was dark like rich chocolate and chased all the way down her spine to her toes.

"Ah, you're learning quick, sweet thing. There's nothing like the perfect mixture of pain and pleasure."

"Colton," she whined. "Please."

He leaned over and kissed her heated, bare flesh. Once again, he smoothed his hand lower and impaled her with two long, skilled fingers. When fully embedded, he pumped in a rapid rhythm, his thumb passing over her anus, sending electrical currents spiking through her lower body. He honed on to her elusive G-spot, finger-fucking her until she could barely contain herself.

She began to fight with him, desperate to join with him intimately, to have his cock penetrating her pussy to relieve the growing need building inside her core. Wiggling and reaching for him was no help against his solid strength holding her in place. Then, without warning, he pulled his fingers free and stood, spilling her onto the ground. On her hands and knees, naked ass kissing the open air, she looked up to him. Colton was a tall man, his gaze hard, and the bulge in his Wranglers was larger than life.

Now, she'd get what she needed. But he didn't step behind her but over her, heading for the staircase.

"Hey! Where do you think you're going?"

"Game's over. I can't do this anymore."

"What!" She struggled to pull up her jeans as he disappeared down the ladder. "Why the hell not?"

She chased after him, out of the barn, as he walked at a brisk clip toward his horse. When he stopped to untie the lead, she grabbed his arm and forced him to pay her notice.

"What's wrong with you? Isn't this what you wanted? Why you came here?" Her breathing was still labored from arousal.

"It was wrong of me to come here by myself." He continued to fuss with the horse and lead, not looking her in the eye. A bat escaping hell didn't move as quickly as he did.

"Without Waylon? Is he your voice, Colton? Can't you enjoy a woman without him?" Her words dripped with venom. She wouldn't be denied. She wouldn't be the one to look desperate when this was what he wanted, not she.

He didn't answer but shrugged nonchalantly.

Just before he mounted the horse, she grabbed his shirt with both hands, forcing him to look at her. "Colton! What did I do wrong?" She'd expected him to flee after he'd gotten what he'd come for, but he hadn't even gotten his belt off before he'd turned and run.

He exhaled heavily from his nose and narrowed his eyes as if assessing her. "You're too good for me, Callie. Be smart and stay away from me." With that, he swung his leg over the saddle and prodded the horse for a hasty retreat. She stood rooted in place for the longest time, watching him disappear over the horizon, not sure if she should feel flattered, rejected, or annoyed—but she certainly felt like a fool.

Callie's traitorous childhood scars bubbled to the surface. Daddy issues? Mommy issues? She only knew that Colton's abandonment hit her hard. That clingy feeling gripped her, telling her to chase after him and beg for his love. But she wasn't that little girl anymore. She prided herself on being a strong, independent woman, unaffected by her past. She'd get through this, even if it killed her.

* * * *

Nearly a week later, Callie was dressing after a shower when she heard movement coming from the living room. Her grandfather was in town having lunch with friends, something that had become a regular occurrence for him. His health had improved greatly as of late, and she was thankful to have him back to his usual self. With him away from home, what was the cause of the noise?

She finished pulling on a fresh T-shirt and towel dried her hair as she quietly padded toward the source of the sound she had heard. Someone was squatting down, his back to her, rooting through the papers that she kept in an old milk crate beside the shelf. She swallowed hard, afraid to breathe and be heard. Ever so carefully, she reversed her steps and returned to her room.

When Callie came back to face the intruder, she was prepared with the nine millimeter she kept under her mattress. A girl could never be too careful living in the middle of nowhere with no man to protect her.

"Stand up!" she ordered with the gun aimed at his blond head. He froze, and then, as if knowing a gun was trained on him, he rose slowly with arms raised. "Turn around."

When she recognized Josh's face, she sunk in relief, but then her suspicions rose significantly. She hadn't seen him since he'd deserted her at the Black ranch weeks earlier. He hadn't come by to deliver feed or help with her fields or even call to apologize. Just seeing her longtime friend after such a betrayal made her trigger finger itchy.

"Callie, I can explain."

"Really? You can explain why you broke into my house?"

"The door wasn't locked."

"That doesn't give you the right to just waltz on in here and snoop through my stuff. And don't try and tell me you came to see me because my grandpa took the truck and you wouldn't have expected me to be home."

"You don't understand. I'm trying to help you. Help us."

"Help us? What on God's green earth are you talking about?"

"I'm looking for your mortgage papers. I don't want you getting in any more trouble than you're in, Callie. We can fix this mess. Together."

"Josh, you're talking crazy. There is no us, no working together. The minute you drove away with my truck destroyed any chance of an us. Besides, my problems are over. The Blacks aren't trying to take over my farm anymore." She may have still felt hatred for Josh, but he was a longtime childhood friend, and part of her hoped to salvage something of their friendship in the future.

"What did you have to do to get them to promise that?"

"That's none of your business!" She flicked the gun, motioning him to the front door. Once she was on the porch and Josh was standing ten feet in front of the house, she continued. "Get off my land, and don't you dare come back."

"Callie, they're lying to you! If you'd just listen to me."

"Go!" Her mind was already whirling. She couldn't think and didn't want to hear any more lies. With shoulders sunk and eyes sad, he returned to his truck. For a brief moment, he reminded her of the old Josh who'd loved and comforted her, but the fleeting feeling passed quickly when she remembered how easily he'd followed Colton and Waylon's instructions to kiss her against her will. Then he'd deserted her with the maniacs.

Once Josh was out of sight and the distant cloud of dust from his truck had settled, she dropped down onto her grandpa's rocking chair. She had tried to forget about Colton, Waylon, and Boyd. Callie farmed, cleaned, cooked, and handled business like before, even more focused, but her heart wasn't in it. Her mind drifted continually to those three rugged cowboys. They consumed her dreams, and she secretly wished they'd show up and sweep her off her feet. All three of them.

But Boyd had had his way with her and never called again. Colton had made it clear he couldn't even stand the sight of her when he'd disappeared without a trace. Waylon didn't seem to act without Colton, and besides, he had a girlfriend. She ground her teeth together, thinking about Sharon holding possession of someone she desperately wanted for her own.

Chapter Sixteen

"You saw her again, didn't you?"

"How do you know?" asked Colton.

Mary Sue snorted an unfeminine sound as she continued to file folders. "You look like you're twelve years old again, all wide-eyed and flush with young love."

"Nonsense."

"I've known you since you were in diapers, Colton. And haven't you confessed many of your wicked deeds to me that you wouldn't dare share with your parents?"

"Mary Sue, I think I'm losing my mind over that girl. Something's not right with me." He pulled out a chair and sat backwards on it. "I went to see her without Waylon, and things were fine at first, but then...I don't know."

"You have feelings for her. Nothing wrong with that."

"Yes, there is." He shook his head. Women didn't affect him. He was Colton Black. Other men would give their left nut to be him. No commitments, all the strings-free one-nighters he could handle, and enough money to buy happiness. Then why did he feel so empty lately? Why did Callie make him feel ashamed to be a womanizer?

"What did you tell me last week?"

Colton sighed. "That I thought I had feelings for her."

"You do. You came to me a mess, or don't you remember? That girl is the best thing that ever happened to you, son. She's forcing you to have a conscience. Only one woman can do that for you."

He looked at her, dumbfounded. Mary Sue cupped both his cheeks, shook her head, and then kissed him on the forehead.

"Handsome as all hell, but not too bright, are you? You're falling in love, Colton Black. The sooner you face that fact, the sooner you'll find peace in your life." Then, just like the enigma she was, Mary Sue disappeared down the hall without another word, leaving him to consider what she'd said.

Love? Colton didn't know love, not in a romantic way. Even during all his past sexual encounters, he'd had to force himself to slow down and consider the women he fucked, or else he was likely to go too far with the BDSM. He'd just never cared until Callie. Could you fall in love after only a couple of weeks, a few encounters? It didn't seem likely, especially for him.

* * * *

It rained for two days nonstop. Callie didn't have time to consider what had happened between Colton and her last week. Their home was in a valley, and the water was making life hell, flooding the kitchen and making the farm a giant mud hole. Her gardens, which she painstakingly cared for and relied on for their meals, were washed away the first day the storms hit. Her grandfather came down with a chest cough that wouldn't cease. The damp, cool air didn't help. He didn't leave his bed, and the town doctor was due to stop by in the evening to check on him. That's if the roads were clear enough.

Callie wore an old checkered shirt over her own as she battled the rain in an attempt to collect her cattle and get them into their holding pen. Some were stuck in the mud. Others were scared off by the lightning. Right now, she wished her friendship with Josh hadn't gone sour, because she didn't have a friend in the world. Rounding up the animals while soaked to the skin, cold and exhausted, was no easy task.

She pulled one boot out of the mud, but the other stuck, making her lose balance and fall to her knees in the thick, dark mud. At that point, she nearly lost it, that tenuous hold on her emotions. But she took a cleansing breath, gritted her teeth, and pulled herself back up. That's when she noticed two shadowy figures on horseback through the blur of rainfall. She squinted, wiping her mop of wet hair back, but couldn't make out the visitors until they were almost on top of her.

"Need some help?" asked Boyd. She scowled. Maybe loving and leaving was commonplace for him, but not for her. She had hoped for more from Boyd, but he'd disappointed her like everyone else.

"No. I don't need any help." She plodded on, pulling one leg out of the mud to move farther away from them. Simultaneously, both Boyd and Waylon dismounted.

"Take her into the barn and out of the rain. I'll round up the rest of the cattle." Boyd spoke with an undeniable authority. With her exhaustion, she didn't continue to argue, but let Waylon lead her back to the barn. She leaned on him for strength until he swept her up into his arms and carried her the rest of the way through the rain and mud. Boyd's voice and whistling in the distance assured her that he knew what he was doing and would have her cattle secured in a fraction of the time it would have taken her.

Once in the shelter of the barn, the static of rainfall on the wooden roof echoed around them. Callie ran her hands through her hair and looked down at herself. Her clothes clung to her, leaving little to the imagination. But then again, Waylon had seen all of her and done amazing things to her body.

"How's Sharon?" She cringed as soon as she asked the question. The words just blurted out before she could stop them.

He narrowed his steely blue eyes and cocked his head. "Sharon? You're soaked and covered in mud, and that's all you can think to ask me?"

"Never mind." She turned away from him, but he spun her around and held both her arms in his capable hands. He ducked to her level and kissed her with enough heat to knock her senseless. His lips were wet from the rain, his chin heavy with stubble, and the feel of his warm lips were no less comforting than an embrace when she desperately needed one. She latched on to his plaid shirt and kissed him back with equal passion. Was she that starved for affection? Callie thought she'd die, wither away, if separated from him now. She pressed into him with the little strength she had left, forcing him to back up against the nearest stall. Pulling the V of his collar, she popped several buttons, exposing the firm, muscled planes of his pecs and his small brown nipples. She wet her lips as liquid heat seemed to fill her body, staving off the cold and releasing into her already soaked panties.

"I broke up with Sharon," he said, taking a breath.

She couldn't hide the little smile that pulled at the corners of her mouth. "Why?" Callie wanted him to tell her sweet nothings. Tell her she was the reason he broke up with his girlfriend. Damn, she just wanted to be special to someone for once in her life. Even if it were a lie.

He growled and gripped both her thighs, heaving her up against his chest. She wrapped her legs around his narrow waist and her arms around his neck. "You are gonna be the death of me, darlin'."

His kiss fueled her desire like lighter fluid to a fire. She squirmed against him as he walked her blindly through the center of the barn, hopefully to fuck her against the nearest wall.

"Cattle are all in their keep and I—" Boyd's deep voice cut off abruptly.

Callie and Waylon both turned their heads in his direction. "I told you you'd be the death of me," whispered Waylon. "I have the feeling both my brothers are equally smitten with you." He lowered her to the ground.

"Didn't you hear me when I warned Colton to stay away from Callie, little brother?" Boyd stalked forward with deadly intent written in his eyes. "I kept telling you not to go man-whoring around with Colton. You didn't listen. Now you've sunk low enough to try and steal my woman from right under my nose?"

"Your woman?" Callie planted her hands on her hips as an unexpected anger filled her veins with venom. "Is this how you treat *your* woman? I haven't seen or heard from you since that night in my room, Boyd. I may look like a stone-cold bitch, but I have feelings. You can't disappear on me and show up expecting to lay a claim."

"I should have called. I should have come back."

"Damn right, you should have." She felt tears sting her eyes, and she forced herself to get a grip, not willing to offer a public display of emotion. "I suppose I should be used to abandonment."

"I'm sorry, Callie. This is new to me." Boyd's stance and eyes softened as he pleaded with her, but the hurt she had pushed away from his casual dismissal started a tidal wave of emotion that threatened to topple her over.

"No! Boyd, do you know what my mother said to my grandma when she handed me over to her? I was only two days old, and she said, 'Take this little bitch off my hands, she'll only ruin my life.'" She cursed herself for revealing the one-liner that had haunted her all her life, made her feel like the worst mistake and a continual burden to those around her. Ever since she'd overheard her deceased aunt and grandma talking on the phone when she was nine years old, she'd held on to those last words from her mother. No child should have to live with that kind of shame and hurt, but she did like a pro, until now.

Callie ran. She ran out the back of the barn and into the rain with no destination in mind except getting away from Boyd, away from the men who were somehow capable of breaking down her barriers and making her the pathetic, weak woman she didn't want to become.

"Callie! Wait!" She wasn't sure which man called her. It didn't matter. She needed space, needed to breath, and needed the rain to cleanse her soul. As she ran, falling in mud and getting back up, the rain began to settle, coming down as a gentle shower with the clouds breaking up above her. When she thought she couldn't go another step, she kept going, running from the ghosts of the past that threatened to unravel her.

She felt them, even before they took her down in the mud. When they caught up with her, breathing heavily, grunting as they both tackled her, she kicked and fought until she expelled her last bit of energy. Finally, all three of them lay in the mud looking up at the clearing sky, glimpses of blue greeting them as the rain tapered off. Callie's outburst brought back her sensibility, and she felt like a fool for how she'd acted in the barn. If only she could wind back time and not make herself appear like a damaged fool of a cowgirl.

* * * *

Waylon was torn in a million pieces. He was close enough with Colton to know that his brother was falling hard for Callie, even if he didn't know it himself. Boyd had already staked a claim on her and told Waylon himself that she had his heart. Who was he to interfere in an already ugly love triangle?

After Callie's painful confession in the barn, Waylon wanted nothing more than to comfort her. He needed to pull her into his arms, not because of lust, but to offer love and comfort. With his life a chaotic menagerie with no anchor, he craved a stable life with Callie. She was a woman of worth and would no doubt appease his raging libido. But how could he compete with his brothers, especially Colton, God's gift to women? Waylon was just the middleman, taking orders from his eldest brother when they played their ménage games with women.

He'd never planned to seduce Callie in the barn. He and Boyd had only come to check up on her due to the heavy rain. Many of their neighbors were flooded out, and they wanted to ensure that she and her grandfather were at least safe. But once he'd had her alone in the barn, his body had erupted in wanton desire for the girl. Even dripping wet and filthy, she was gorgeous, naturally perfect, and he kissed her on impulse. When she hadn't refused him but spurred him on, he'd been ready to fuck her right there against the wall of the barn. Now, things couldn't be more complicated.

Chapter Seventeen

Boyd was the first to sit up. Callie and Waylon still lay on the earth, exposed flesh covered in a brown film and clothes soaked and filthy. The sight of numerous entwining limbs was oddly erotic, but he pushed the thought away.

"Callie, I'm sorry for staying away. I'm not like your mother or father." He leaned over her, a hand supporting his weight on either side of her head. "I'm not going anywhere," he whispered.

She closed her eyes and took a deep breath, which forced her ample breasts to press up against his chest for a moment. "Please, just forget that happened. I don't know what came over me."

He used his thumb to remove a patch of mud from her cheek, only smearing it more, which made him laugh. His laughter must have been contagious, especially when they all looked a sight. He dropped back to the ground, and they each found the humor in the madness.

"What the hell happened here?" A few minutes later, Colton dismounted his horse and stood over them with arms crossed over his chest like a disapproving father.

"Long story. Help me up." Colton leant Boyd his arm and tugged him out of the suction of mud. He felt heavy and craved nothing more than a dip in the pond behind their ranch. Instead, he peeled off his shirt and tossed it with disregard. What he didn't expect was the way Callie devoured his bare upper body with the same lust in her eyes that she'd had when they made love. He wished they were alone so he could confess his feelings to her and show her by making sweet love to her for hours. It had been a foolish move to stay away from her. With the conflict between him and Colton, he thought some time apart from Callie, the source of their rivalry, would shed some light on the subject. It only made him want her more. If he'd ever expected she'd think he'd deserted her, abandoned her like some cheap one-night stand, he would have returned to her the very next day. He sure had a lot to learn about relationships, and that's exactly what he wanted from Callie—a relationship, a future, a family.

"Road's closed. The only way around is by horseback, and even that's a pain in the ass with the mud. When you head back, go through the forest, it's not as bad as the fields." Colton reached out to help Callie up. Once up, she stripped off her outer shirt, leaving a thin cotton T-shirt clinging to her breasts and riding up past her belly button. Damn, the woman had a body to kill for. The way Colton and Waylon observed her with unblinking focus meant they felt the same way as he.

"I'll bring Callie home and join you both in a minute," said Boyd, not wanting to give either brother a moment alone with her.

"No! I can't go home like this. Our plumbing and electricity is shot. The generator's only keeping the essentials on, and I need a shower in the worst way. Can't I come to your place and get cleaned up a bit? Then maybe use your phone to call someone to come do repairs?"

Before she even finished talking, Colton mounted the black stallion and closed the short distance between him and Callie. "Come on, sweet thing." He held out his arm, and she gratefully swung herself up behind him and wrapped her arms around his waist. Boyd wished it were he in his brother's place feeling her arms wrapped around his body and her soft breasts pressed against his back. He growled his disapproval and slopped through the mud to retrieve his own horse, followed by Waylon, who had been quiet since Boyd had found him kissing Callie in the barn.

* * * *

"Take your clothes off," said Colton. He sat on a folding metal chair in the large shower room meant for the ranch hands who lived in the portables out back. Only his shirt was dirty from where Callie had leaned into him on the horse ride back to his place, but he quickly lost it, sitting back in the chair bare-chested and sexier than sin. He regarded her with a controlled interest. She stood in the sterile, empty, tiled room covered in mud that continued to dry to her skin, making her feel itchy and uncomfortable.

"Aren't you going to leave first?" He wasn't just going to sit there and watch her undress, was he?

"I'm not going anywhere, sweet thing. Take your clothes off. Everything. Bra and panties, too."

Something about Colton made her want to obey him. Normally, she loved confrontations, opportunities to display her dominant personality. With Colton, she wanted to let it all go, trust him to lead her wherever he chose. The thought of getting naked in front of him made her pussy weep and nipples tighten beneath her cotton bra.

She complied, fighting her jeans down her hips and kicking them off with her boots. Next came her shirt, leaving her in just her undergarments. His interest increased, and he sat straighter in the chair. He nodded once for her to continue, resting his elbows on his knees. The room felt so big and empty, making her feel more vulnerable than ever. She unclasped her bra and slid it slowly down her arms, freeing her generous breasts. They'd always been a burden to her and attracted unwanted attention when she had to deal with cowboys day in, day out. However, the burning lust in Colton's eyes as he studied her curves made her proud.

She shimmied out of her panties, which was the hardest step, leaving her completely nude before him.

"You're a dirty girl, Callie." He stood, the leather of his boots creaking as he rose to his full height, towering over her. As he approached, he licked his lips, but again, his eyes remained void of emotion. They were deep blue pools to get lost in, to forget everything in except his control.

She swallowed the lump in her throat as he led her to the tiled wall and turned on one of the showerheads. He held her aside as he tested the temperature with the other hand until he believed it was perfect.

"Get under the water." She obeyed, standing under the warm, powerful spray. It felt good, soothing. The brown water circled around her before going down the nearest drain. Colton's boots were getting soaked, as were his Wranglers, but he didn't appear to mind— he was too busy soaping up his hands. When he placed those hands, slippery but calloused, over her breasts, she gasped. He continued to lather up her body with sensual skill, not touching her where she needed him most. Her pussy throbbed, and she continually replayed their last encounter in her head, when he'd impaled her with his long, sinful fingers. She hated him for running out on her that day, just as all men seemed to do, but now, she was thankful for the moment. With Colton, she expected that these few blessed moments were all she'd get. The realization saddened her. She wanted it all but had nothing but brief memories to cling to.

Callie couldn't hold back. Her desire continued to build inside her, stoked by Colton's every touch. She reached out, running her hands up from his stomach, over his chest, to his shoulders. Every inch of him was hard, all male, and she reveled in the feel of him.

"Colton..."

"I know I'm bad for you, but I can't seem to be able to stay away. Guess that makes me the worst kind of bastard." His voice was laced with regret.

"I want you to want me. I don't want you to stay away," she whispered, afraid of her own admission. She wanted Colton just as much as she did Boyd and Waylon, just in a different way. He was sex on a stick, dark and mysterious. She wanted him to dominate her...love her.

He trailed his hands around her to cup her ass, giving a squeeze and pulling her tightly against him.

"You don't know what you're asking, darlin'. I'll eat a sweet thing like you alive." He leaned down to inhale her scent, as if trying to remember her essence because he was leaving her for good. She felt him mentally pull away, as if he consciously made the decision to put her needs before his desire to fuck her. It terrified her. Callie was tired of abandonment, and she wasn't the fragile woman he thought her to be. She was strong inside and out, a woman used to manual labor and dealing with riffraff. Anything he could dish out sexually, she could take, wanted to take.

In a desperate attempt, she grabbed his belt and started to pull the leather out of the buckle. He stilled her hands. "Don't, Callie. I'm not good at this on my own. I won't be able to keep control."

He referred to Waylon, his middleman in the sex games. Why did he need him? Was he afraid to really let loose, to feel, rather than just fuck?

"I don't care." She rose up on her tiptoes, her body now thoroughly cleansed. "Please kiss me."

She teased his lower lip with her tongue, pulling him down to her level.

He exhaled, then kissed her exactly how she wanted, needed. Nothing sweet or gentle about him—he was raw passion and strength, an inferno of desire waiting to erupt. He nipped her lips, then her jawline, backing her up to the cold, ceramic tiled wall. She shuddered as the coolness penetrated her back and Colton's heat seared her from the front. As they kissed, she continued to unbuckle him, and this time, he didn't protest.

"You're too good for me, Callie," he muttered between kisses.

"Stop saying that." Once she'd unbuckled and unzipped, she slipped her hand into his jeans, seeking out the erection she felt prodding her stomach. The man was hard as steel. She'd feel every thick inch of him filling her. Her pussy throbbed in anticipation, her folds dripping with arousal.

When she released his cock and wrapped her fingers around it, he grunted. "Jesus Christ, Callie. You're killing me."

Just then, the double doors to the shower room burst open, revealing two filthy cowboys.

"You just couldn't wait, could you, Colton?" Waylon, Colton's sexual teammate, entered the room, stripping as he walked. Callie's arousal rose significantly. All these men who held her heart and desires were wickedly attractive, with bodies built for sex. Boyd remained silent by the now-closed doors. He tossed his soiled cowboy hat in a corner, raised his chin, and squared his shoulders. She remembered how naked she was.

"I guess you could join in. We'll finish what we started with this young filly," said Colton, not offended, but apparently comfortable sharing with Waylon. The thought of taking both men sent erotic thrills zinging through her clit. The unknown, the anticipation, the surrender—it all sent her to a new plane of sensation.

Chapter Eighteen

Waylon had shown up just in time. When he and Boyd hadn't found Colton in the house, he knew his brother would bring Callie here. They thought too much alike. Seeing her naked, her beautiful curves bare and tempting, had him stripping his clothes in a hurry. He was surprised to see Colton kissing Callie—he always avoided such intimacy—but then again, he knew his brothers both had deep feelings for the sexy little blonde.

Colton seemed to switch to game mode once Waylon entered the picture. He pulled away from Callie, leaving her standing alone and naked under the spray of water. His brother took a seat on the metal bench along the opposite wall, no doubt waiting for Waylon to accept his first order. Right now, the last thing on his mind was games. He wanted to pull Callie into his arms and kiss her like there was no tomorrow. He wanted to promise her the world and mean it. She was so much more than a toy. He hoped his brothers knew what they were playing with.

"Waylon?" she questioned.

"You ready for some games, Callie?" he asked, while approaching her tentatively in just his damp boxers. His cock wept with the need to penetrate her tight pussy. He remembered exactly how she tasted with vivid detail. Just the thought made him harder still, and she didn't fail to notice as her eyes darted low.

Her breathing quickened, her lips were parted to supply her starved lungs with more oxygen. "Maybe."

"No maybes, darlin'. You're gonna obey, or else you'll be punished. Don't you remember the rules?"

He could see her swallow the nervous lump in her throat, but her eyes were wide and eager.

"Touch yourself. Squeeze those beautiful tits, and pinch your pretty little nipples." He waited for her to comply. "Go on."

Biting her lower lip, her cheeks turning a heated pink, she reached up and cupped her own breasts. She toyed with her nipples until her eyes took on a bedroom haze, and he knew she was well on her way to being prepared for them. All of them. The brief eye contact he shared with Colton told him that he planned to invite Boyd to this party. When Colton nodded to him, he understood what to do next.

"Good girl. Now I want you to unbuckle Boyd's belt, squat down, and suck his cock. Guarantee you it'll be good and hard for you."

Boyd frowned. "I never said I was joining in."

"I also haven't seen you making your usual territorial show over Callie. Stop denying yourself, brother. It's about time you joined us."

Before Boyd could argue, Callie followed the direction, prancing over to him. Boyd didn't stop her when she fiddled with his belt. The man needed to shower in the worst way, just as he did. While Waylon waited for Callie to get Boyd's pants down, he took the opportunity to let the water flowing from the showerhead rush down his body, cleansing away the muddy film. He shook his dirty-blond hair and rubbed his palm over his aching erection.

"Callie, you don't have to do this," said Boyd.

Colton spoke up. "Yes, she does. If she doesn't obey, I'll spank her myself." His voice was deep from arousal.

Boyd frowned, opening his mouth to shout back some choice words, but swallowed whatever he was going to say when Callie's lips wrapped around his dick. He almost fell back from the unexpected rush of pleasure. One hand braced the wall behind him while he dug the other through Callie's damp blonde hair.

"What do ya know, Colton? I think he likes it." Waylon chuckled as he watched the erotic act, which, surprisingly, pleased him as much as he knew it pleased Boyd. He wondered how his brother would react once Waylon told Callie to perform acts on him or Colton. Would he be able to handle it or blow up in a possessive rage? Time would tell because it was about time Waylon tapped that ass himself. He'd waited long enough, dreamed of fucking Callie every way until Sunday. He knew how tight her pussy would be. Getting a standard dildo inside her had been difficult, even with her overflow of moisture to help.

* * * *

Boyd dropped his head back, eyes closed, as he absorbed the feeling of Callie's hot mouth and lively tongue devouring his cock hungrily. Since her almost-attempt to give him a blow job in the diner, he'd needed this, dreamed of this. She sucked him with enthusiasm, even making sexy little mewling sounds and cupping his balls with her free hand as she pumped his shaft in time with her sucking. Knowing his brothers stood just off in the distance watching every detail of their private act added to the eroticism. He'd never expected to experience a thrill from the public display of affection. Maybe there was something to their games after all—no, it had to do with the woman. Callie made all the difference.

"That's enough, darlin'. The night's young, and we don't want him coming just yet," said Waylon after a few minutes of ecstasy.

"The hell we don't!" Boyd tightened his grip in Callie's hair, not willing to end the rush of heat reaching all the way to his testicles. His own kin would rob him of an orgasm?

"Callie. There're three of us. Colton's waiting for you on the bench."

Callie released Boyd's cock and stood to follow Waylon's direction. What the fuck? He didn't like the game when it didn't include him. Callie appeared to be enjoying herself, but could he watch her suck another man's dick in front of him, even if it was his brother's?

He watched her full, round ass sway side to side as she crossed the room to the bench where Colton sat. Waylon disappeared from the room, so he took his place under the warm stream of water now making the room cloud with humidity. He heard a truck door slam before Waylon rejoined them and closed the door to the shower room shut. In his hand was a small black bag.

"All right, darlin'. Do you trust us?" asked Waylon, settling near the bench.

She nodded, her eyes flitting to each man.

"Good. I'm gonna tie you up. Not like last time, just your wrists."

"Is that necessary?" asked Boyd. He felt the need to defend Callie, even though she didn't look like she needed to be saved. If he were any sort of gentleman, he'd haul Callie out of there and offer her some fucking dignity. Then why didn't he? He prided himself on the values his father had raised him with, beat into him, but right now, all he wanted to do was allow his mind and body to float in the humid mist and absorb the erotic energy in the room. Yes, he wasn't a blood brother to Colton and Waylon, but that fact wasn't what separated them. The one factor keeping them separate was that his brothers had a connection through their sexual games. Though Boyd had never been interested, things changed now because of Callie. She could be the uniting factor to bring them closer together as brothers. Fool thoughts, but right now, his cock seemed to control his actions.

"Get me the rope out of my bag," said Waylon.

His younger brother positioned Callie over the bench, her bare pussy straddling the wood, and then he shackled her wrists with a pair of red handcuffs in front of her.

Boyd dug through the bag filled with an array of sex toys and pulled the thin white rope free from the other items. Waylon snagged it from him as soon as he could reach and proceeded to tie the cuffs to the head of the bench with the rope. She had lots of slack and freedom. If she tried, she'd even be able to reach her bound hands above her head. His curiosity was piqued.

"Very good." Waylon ran his palm down Callie's backbone. When he reached her ass, he gave her a sharp swat.

"What was that for?" she asked angrily.

"Just testing." He smirked, and Boyd didn't fail to notice the connection passing through their eye contact. Was it possible Callie had feelings for his brothers? Was it possible that his brothers were falling in love with the same woman who already held his heart?

"She likes getting spanked. Don't you, sweet thing?" Colton straddled the bench behind her in just his blue jeans. He whispered against the side of her neck and pushed the weight of his body into her back. Boyd remained rooted in place, unable to move or speak, only capable of watching.

"Colton. Don't tease me." Callie whined and dropped her head back against Colton's shoulder. Her breasts heaved as she gasped for air. He'd assume the woman was being tortured, but he could practically feel the lust pouring out of her. The scent of sex filled the humid space, making Boyd's cock ache. He wanted Callie's lips back around his swollen head, sucking, licking.

"Boyd. Strip off your jeans and get in front of your woman." Like a robot, he complied. He wasn't one to take an order, but right now, he was entranced by the game.

He straddled the bench facing Callie, his ramrod-hard dick knocking on the metal as he sat. She hooked her bound hands around his neck and pulled herself to his mouth. Her eyes were glazed over, promising him anything and everything. He kissed her, sucking on her lips and tongue, savoring her taste and texture. She nipped his lip, and he hissed through his teeth.

Callie pushed him down with force, but he realized it was actually Colton's weight bringing her forward. He lay back on the cool metal, his legs splayed on either side of the bench, his cock a virile arrow pointing straight to the ceiling. When Callie leaned over and licked the pre-cum off his cock, sending a violent shiver through his body, she squealed and pulled back, leaving him wanting for more. Colton's arms snaked around her and pinched her nipples.

"Waylon didn't tell you to suck cock, did he?"

"No."

Waylon took over. He brushed the damp hair off Callie's face and gave her a kiss to the forehead. "What you're going to do is sit on Boyd's cock, not suck it. Can you handle that, darlin'?"

She smiled at Boyd, like a fox about to enter the chicken coop, and melted his heart. It was just the two of them at that moment. Even with both his brothers watching eagerly, somehow, it didn't bother him when he looked in Callie's cornflower-blue eyes.

Waylon passed him a condom package. "Put this on yourself, I ain't helping you."

As Boyd sheathed himself, Callie moved into position, straddling his lap. His cock throbbed, so filled with blood he felt he'd explode if she didn't impale herself over him soon.

She supported herself with her bound hands against his chest, the metal of the thin chain clanging as she wiggled into position. "Help me, Boyd." He reached down and supported his cock in his fist as Callie lowered herself over his rigid length.

"Oh, fuck," he muttered as her heat enveloped him. She was so tight, so wet, and so perfect. He closed his eyes and absorbed the pleasure flowing through his system. Waylon laughed—a low, throaty sound of approval.

"Your turn, Colton," said Waylon.

Boyd was too lost in the sexual bliss of Callie working his cock, up and down, up and down. She rose up on her feet until just his thick head remained within her body, then slammed down until she buried it to the hilt. The moans he made with each pass were impossible to hold back.

A new sound escaped Callie's lips, making him open his eyes. Colton held her from behind, trailing kisses along her neck and shoulder. "Lean forward, sweet thing. You've done this already. I know you can handle it."

Callie dropped forward, the new position squeezing his cock harder. Boyd heard the spurt of lube being squeezed from a tube and the crinkle of a wrapper, and then Callie's breathing picked up. "That's a girl. Relax."

"I'm scared, Colton." Her voice was barely a whisper. "I don't think I can fit two cocks inside me."

Chapter Nineteen

Callie felt a mixture of fear and excitement, a heady combination. She'd had a dildo in her anus, thanks to Colton and Waylon, but never a man's penis, and never at the same time as she rode a second cock. Even though adrenaline spiked through her blood, she couldn't say no. She wanted this. The idea of having Boyd, the man she was falling in love with, and Colton, the man she wanted to possess, fucking her simultaneously nearly brought her to orgasm.

"You don't have to do this, sweetheart." Boyd held her face in his warm hands and kissed her. She saw the war raging in his eyes. He wanted her to fuck him and his brother at the same time, but he wouldn't allow her if it wasn't exactly what she wanted, too. Callie wouldn't squander this opportunity. The fact that Boyd was participating in his brothers' games, sharing her, was monumental. This was everything she could have hoped for.

"No. I want you both. All three of you, actually." She stretched out her bound hands above her and rested her cheek against Boyd's chest. As she clenched her pussy around his thick cock, he groaned his appreciation. "Do it, Colton. Fuck me before I change my mind."

The cool jolt from his lube-covered dick pressed against her ass. She tried to relax, loosen her unforgiving sphincter muscles for his penetration. As he forced his cock deeper, he reached around between her and Boyd and massaged her clit. She clenched her teeth as he inched his way deeper into her ass. Boyd moaned as the second penis filled her, squeezing his limited space within her body.

"Damn, that's fucking amazing," Boyd muttered as he smoothed his hands up and down her sides. His touch sizzled through her senses, pulling her deeper into the erotic bliss consuming her.

"I told you you didn't know what you were missing," said Waylon, slapping his brother on the shoulder.

"Colton…" she whined, wiggling against him. He moved agonizingly slowly. She knew he tried not to hurt her, even though she doubted he gave other women such tenderness. Being wanted, being cared for, in addition to the mind-blowing sex, made her clit pulse and heat, so close to orgasm. The discomfort had already passed, and she wanted all of him buried inside her, both cocks, both men.

"You okay, sweet thing?" asked Colton.

"More. I want more." She rocked her pelvis, sending electric waves of desire swirling through her pussy, her ass.

The men began to work her like a finely tuned machine. She pulled herself up to her elbows as Boyd secured her by the hips, fighting for space with Colton's hands and limbs. Having both men fill her was incomparable. She was stretched to the limit, able to feel both cocks rubbing inside her, creating delicious friction. Then she thought of Waylon.

He choreographed the game, doled out the explicit instructions. When did he get to play? She wanted all the Black brothers without forgetting about the youngest. Waylon was nothing to scoff at—tall, lean-muscled, with a face so handsome he belonged on the cover of *GQ* magazine. "Waylon. Join us. Please."

He stood next to her, oblivious to the men fucking her, and stroked her hair. She licked her lips and eyed the bulge in his wet boxer briefs. Knowing exactly what she wanted, he pulled the material down to his thighs and moved close enough that she could capture him with her lips. His taste exploded in her mouth, all male. She let out her sexual energy on his thick cock, sucking, tasting, and lapping with enthusiasm. When Boyd or Colton pushed her harder, she responded by sucking Waylon deeper down her throat. All four of them were joined, one unit, a single experience. She never wanted the ecstasy to end but held back her orgasm in hopes of enjoying her men for even a few minutes longer.

"Shit, Callie. You're tight. So fucking tight. Come for me, darlin'." Colton bit down on the muscle at the base of her neck, and the jolt of pain released the orgasm that had been waiting below the surface. It rocketed through her with enough power and energy to lift her to another plane of existence. She cried out, pulling off Waylon's penis and dropping her head to Boyd's chest.

"Oh, my God!" Callie's body turned pliant, boneless, as she collapsed her full weight against Boyd. She felt Colton's cock swell before his release. While she continued to milk Boyd's cock, he joined his brother. Both men growled, masculine sounds filling the steamy room. Waylon stroked his length with a clenched fist, pumping with vigor as he tried to reach his peak. His jaw was set, and his eyes blazed with lust as he watched her, watching him.

A moment later, Waylon came. The white spray of ejaculate covered his fist and shot outwards to the tiled floor. He dropped to his knees, pressing his forehead against Callie's. "Good?"

"Incredible."

* * * *

Waylon promised to drop by to help Callie with some repairs. After three days since their ménage à quatre, she missed the Black brothers. She'd cleaned most of the muck around her place from the storm, and the land was no longer a muddy mess. A plumber had come to her house the day after she left the brothers with orders to fix anything necessary, no charge to Callie. Her first instinct was to refuse the charity, but she reminded herself that they weren't buying her love or her body. She'd already offered herself to them freely.

Anything done for her after their sexual act was because they wanted to do it.

Callie had been out to the feed store earlier. Apparently, it was Jack Smith acting for the Black Corporation, not the brothers themselves, who had forced Mr. McGraw to sign the repo papers for her horses. Now that things had been straightened out, life slowly returned to normal. Unfortunately, normal meant that she was still broke as ever.

She had finished doing her morning chores around the house and had been playing with the dogs, contemplating taking a ride on Paddy. That was until she heard a truck rumble down the long drive to her house. A black pickup truck. After parking, Waylon hopped out with a wide smile on his face. The morning light highlighted the blond in his hair and made his eyes shine bluer than the sky.

"Mornin'."

"All by yourself today?"

"Just me. You disappointed?"

The dogs circled him as he approached her, not snarling because her spirits were high, but cautious of the stranger. When they got too close, he bent low and warned them away with a deep, baritone command. To her surprise, they obeyed and gave him space.

"Wow, even dogs listen to you. I thought your powers only worked on women."

"Hey, that's not fair." He cupped her face and gave her a soft, deep kiss on the lips and then pulled back. "I only have the most honorable intentions when it comes to you."

She scoffed and pulled back. "Sure, Waylon. Just like Colton, right?"

"Maybe. Both my brothers are lovesick, did you know that?" He tagged her arm so she couldn't move farther away. "How does it make you feel to have three grown men irrevocably in love with you?"

"Cut it out." She tried to free herself from his grip.

"No. I'm serious, Callie." The dogs started with a low growl, but Waylon countered with one of his own, silencing them. "Does it make you happy, scared, confused? What?"

"What do you want me to say, Waylon?" Was he trying to trap her? Trying to spell out that she was the worst kind of whore, playing with men's emotions?

"Just answer the question."

"Confused. Happy. Sad. I don't know." She whirled around, freeing her arm, and began pacing the long, unkempt grass. "Waylon, what can happen between us, between the four of us?" She wasn't being smart, she really wanted an answer. Allowing herself to develop feelings for three brothers was emotional suicide. They lived in the Bible Belt, where traditional families were the norm. Three men and one woman never lived happily ever after. They'd be a freak show, even if each one of them agreed to an unorthodox relationship.

"I know I want more than games. I know that I'm tired of bowing out to my brothers."

Callie shook her head. "Waylon, we haven't even been intimate. Not the way I want, anyway. All you do is call the shots. Is that all I can expect from you? A man should have a mind of his own and take what he wants." The way he stared her down with his killer good looks made her womb cramp and twist uncomfortably. She wanted him to take charge and not care about the consequences. Callie wanted Waylon to finish what he'd started with her in the barn, joining them as she had with the other two brothers.

"Be careful what you ask for." A wicked grin pulled at his mouth. "I've been wanting you for myself for weeks now." He reached out and tugged her forward by the loops in her jeans, crashing her against his erection. "Since you like dominant men, I'm going to give you more than you can handle. It's about time I enjoyed you for myself."

"Waylon," she whispered, too turned on to think of a coherent sentence. Callie had learned in a hurry that she liked her men rough and in control when it came to sex. The revelation surprised her when she had always valued her independence and strength. There was just something so primal and erotic about obeying lurid orders and engaging in acts out of her wildest imagination. The final ingredient was trust. She knew her Black men would never hurt her. Even when she was bound and vulnerable, they'd never truly harm her. If she told them to stop at any point, she was confident that they would.

"Where's your grandpa at?" he asked.

"I don't know. He was gone when I got back from the feed store. Probably in town with his friends."

"Good. Because I have a little fantasy I want to play out with you."

She held her breath, excited and anxious as desire grew inside her, making her flush. "Like what?"

"Since I spend a lot of time behind the wheel of my truck, I want to have some enticing memories of that bench seat. I can already picture you laid over the driver's side seat with my cock in your ass."

Callie swallowed hard and tried to contain the inferno building in her pussy. Already, she was wet and ready for Waylon to satisfy any fantasy he had.

"What are you waiting for?"

His adorable grin returned, and he pulled her by the hand to his truck. She couldn't imagine having sex in the wide open area by the front of her house. It may be deserted, but it was still in full public view if anyone happened to ride or drive up to the property. The mere idea of being caught made their illicit act that much more titillating.

"I want you buck-naked, Callie." He opened the driver's side door wide and crowded her into the space it made.

"What if I don't listen?"

"Colton may have been in control before, but it's just me now, darlin'. Who do you think has the bag of toys? Do you think I'm afraid to use a riding crop on your tender pussy?"

She gasped as currents bolted through her clit, preparing her for Waylon's assault. Without another word, she spared no time in removing every stitch of clothing until she stood barefoot on the cool grass and naked as a jaybird in the front of her house.

"Good girl. Now stay put." He reached in the locked box in his truck bed and retrieved the same black bag he'd had in the shower room. "We're gonna have a little fun before I fuck you senseless."

She wanted to scream for him to take her now, no waiting. Her pussy was swollen, ripe, and ready for his invasion, and the thought of waiting made her fidgety and needy.

"Ever use one of these, sweetheart?" He pulled out a pink phallus from his bag, about four inches long, made of firm silicone. After hitting a switch at the base, it began to vibrate in his hand. She trembled, anticipating him using the toy on her body. "Hop up in the driver's seat and keep your legs facing me."

She did as he asked of her. Once seated, Waylon spread her legs apart, and he coaxed her to the edge of the leather. He licked the end of the plastic cock to moisten it while maintaining eye contact with her, and then he used it to spread her folds.

"You're already wet, darlin'. You like being told what to do, don't you?" He plunged the vibrating dildo into her cunt, holding it in just the right position to hit her clit at the same time as it invaded her body. Pumping the toy, he leaned forward and sucked her nipple into his mouth, teasing her with his blunt teeth. She wanted to fall back and let him have his way, but he demanded she watch and sit with her legs parted.

"No more," she cried. The vibrator brought an unnatural intensity to her clit, making her body jolt and shudder. It was sweet torture, and she knew she couldn't bear it much longer.

"I'm testing you. If you pass, I'll fuck you proper. If you fail, you'll get some punishment." He left the vibrator in place and pulled a new riding crop out from under the bench seat. "Ah, ah. Don't move, or I'll have to tie you up again." He tickled her clit with the tip of the riding crop, looking too pleased with himself, while she was going insane from the menagerie of new sensations.

"What test?" she blurted.

"You're not allowed to come until I give you permission." Ha! That would be impossible with his current invasion. She barely held it together as it was. If she could just kiss him, maybe she could melt his resolve and gain some control.

She pulled him closer by the shoulders. "Kiss me, Waylon."

"Soon."

He watched her with an intense interest for more than a minute, like a man possessed. Then he pulled the toy from her pussy, clicked it off, and tossed it behind her. He stood on the running board, unzipped his pants, and freed his cock.

Callie sighed as relief was near. After sheathing himself, he grabbed her hips in a firm lock and thrust his cock into her hot cunt, so ready for him. She cried out as he entered her, and the wave of pleasure took her by storm. Waylon wasn't gentle, but he wasn't brutal, either. He fucked her hard and fast with an untiring energy. She grabbed the back of the bench seat with one hand and the steering wheel with the other. As he began to shudder, close to orgasm, he pulled his cock free and hopped down off the truck. "Flip over." His voice was rough and gravelly, controlled by his animalistic desire.

Callie began to twist, but he flipped her himself, too impatient to wait. Her breasts crushed into the driver's seat, and her ass pointed out the door. Waylon scissored his cock up and down her folds and anus, sending shivers skittering along her exposed flesh. She felt his cock press her nether hole, and she tightened on instinct. "Sorry, sweetheart. I'm taking you up the ass right now. It's all I've dreamt of since I watched Colton fuck you from behind." His cock forged its way into her anus with unforgiving thrusts. She cried out from the momentary shock of pain, which quickly subsided. Once it was fully seated in her ass, she rocked into him, moaning and ready to beg if need be.

"Fuck me, Waylon!"

He growled and did as she asked, fucked her hard while gripping her hips with big, strong cowboy hands. She clawed the leather interior, desperate to cling to something as he rocked her body mercilessly. Every stroke of his cock in her tight rear end forced her clit to rub against the firm leather upholstery. She wanted to come, she felt that heavenly bliss just waiting to erupt, but she forced it away until Waylon gave her the permission she sought.

"Jesus Christ! You're fucking perfect." A few more strong thrusts of his hips. "Now, Callie. Come for me, darlin'." Those simple words were all it took for her orgasm to detonate within her, rocking her walls and surging through her pussy with enough strength to pull the seed from Waylon's cock. He groaned as he pumped his release inside her.

Chapter Twenty

Waylon could barely catch his breath. No woman could drive him crazy the way Callie could. She was so willing, such a perfect woman for him to play with.

He helped her re-dress. When finished, he sat on the open tailgate and pulled her onto his lap. Her skin was sweat-glistened from sex, her lips still swollen from desire. He tucked her close to his body and kissed her. A slow, sensual kiss with promises attached. They'd had their fun, and he wasn't ready to run. No, this was just the beginning. Callie wasn't only a game or toy to him, but so much more. He felt ready to explode, ready to scream from the roof of the house that he loved this woman and couldn't wait to plan their life together.

"There're so many things I want to give you, Callie." He did. He wanted to build her a house with his own two hands, buy her pretty clothes, and make sure she wanted for nothing. His mind raced with possibilities, and for the first time in his life, he was excited about the future.

"I don't need things. Just love. Can you give me your heart and promise not to take it back?" Her tone of voice suggested that she expected to be denied, which only made him desperate to prove his intentions to her. Yes, he liked sex—loved sex. How could he not, with a buxom beauty like Callie? But he wanted her for more than just thrills.

"It's all yours, sweetheart. My heart, my body, everything." He lowered them to the ground. "Enough of this. If we both feel the same way, then I want to move forward. Today." Why wait when they could jump into a life together now? Why should she have to suffer another day in that rundown house with too many bills to pay? He had a bank account with more than he could dream of spending in several lifetimes.

She hesitated. "Waylon, listen to yourself. Who do you sound like?" He puzzled the question in his head until the answer slapped him in the face. His brothers. How the hell would he deal with them? He'd had the biggest revelation of his life, ready to commit for the long haul, but had forgotten that his brothers were equally obsessed with the pretty cowgirl.

He massaged behind his neck and released a tense breath. "I'm going to head back and talk with them. I'll ride down here tonight."

After a final kiss, he boarded his truck and headed back to face the music. It was time for him to be a man and fight for what he wanted.

* * * *

Callie returned to her duties around the farm, which never seemed to end. She still felt the warmth and ease from her orgasm, and her heart smiled with the love shown to her by the Black brothers. When she heard the truck pull up to the front of the house, she smiled, more than willing for another round of sex with Waylon. But as she turned the back corner of the house, the truck wasn't black, but white. Another followed—Josh's old truck. She narrowed her eyes in suspicion and stiffened her posture as she went to meet her uninvited company.

"What do you think you're doing on my property?" she hollered when she saw Jack Smith and two men empty the white truck. If she never saw that pervert again, it would be too soon, and he had the nerve to show up at her front door.

"Callie, I have to talk to you." Josh ran up to her, pulling her to the side as Jack continued on to the back of her property with the men wearing orange construction vests.

"What's going on here? Explain it to me right now!" She crossed her arms stubbornly over her chest. Josh looked so humbled, nervous, even.

"Callie, I tried to stop them. Those Black brothers weren't after your land to expand. They're after the oil under the property." He gave her a jostle. "Don't you see? They've been playing you all along, earning your trust for their strike."

"What strike? What are you talking about?"

"The Blacks took your land, Callie. Didn't you ask for any paperwork when they promised things would be okay? Please don't tell me you took their crooked word for it?"

"I don't understand. The bank stopped calling." Her anger fizzled, and fear crept into her system.

"Doesn't matter. It's all theirs now. Forget about those womanizing assholes and come home with me. I'll take care of you, Callie. Your grandpa's already at my place having lunch with my daddy. It'll all be fine, you'll see."

"How is it fine?" How could everything be over? Her fight, her grandpa's legacy? The enemy had won, and she had to just walk away with her tail between her legs? More importantly, how could the Blacks betray her? She'd believed every word they'd said. They had pulled her into a state of trust and compliance while the deadline for her to pay her taxes came and went as they planned. Bastards! How could she expect three hot, gorgeous cowboys used to having any woman they chose to suddenly want to settle down after knowing her a few weeks? She was nobody, just a simple cowgirl with a couple of dollars to her name. What a fool she'd been. She wanted to kick some serious ass!

"I'm not going home with you," she said. Just because she was in a terrible predicament didn't mean she'd fall into any man's arms. Josh wasn't her savior. He'd had his chance. Now her anger built inside her as she recalled all the nasty things she'd done with those three men. They'd used her and taken advantage of her innocence.

She wanted to scream and stomp, even empty her rifle into the air, but she kept calm. A bomb waiting to explode.

"I love you, Callie. Always have. I understand those Black brothers fooled you, but I can forgive and forget." He forced a kiss on her unexpectedly. "Let's get married. Today."

"What? No! Josh, just stop, I need to think." She fished in her pocket for her truck keys and bolted for her pickup. In a violent spray of gravel, she left her home, maybe for the last time.

* * * *

Colton sat on the sofa with a chilled beer. He'd finished branding a new generation of cattle in the morning and was due to unwind for a while. Waylon came in like a hurricane, insisting he talk with him and Boyd. Mary Sue joined in, eager to hear the important news.

"Okay, let's have it," said Colton.

"It's about Callie."

Boyd massaged his temples and leaned over his knees. "Not again. I'm tired of arguing."

"Listen. I've made a decision, and you all need to hear it." Waylon took a deep breath, and Colton was interested to see where this conversation was going. "I want to marry Callie."

"What?" Colton and Boyd said the same thing at the exact same time, both standing to attention.

"You heard me. I love her, and nothing either of you say is gonna change that. If either of you loved her as you claim, you would have made your move already."

Colton set his beer down on the end table and stepped closer to his youngest brother. "So that's it? That's your big news?"

"Yeah."

Colton chuckled and shook his head. "Think again, hotshot. She ain't yours for the taking."

Mary Sue motioned the three men to take seats. They obeyed her without question. "You three boys are blinder than all, aren't you?" She paced the room between the spaces where the brothers sat. "Can't you see? You all love her. She loves you. I've never seen any one of you happier since she came storming in that fine morning. But for some reason, you're denying yourselves that happiness."

"How can we be happy if only one of us can have her?" asked Boyd.

"Did she choose? I doubt that. If you'd open your eyes, you'd see that there's enough love for all four of you. It may not be the norm around these parts, but since when did any of you boys play by the rules?"

"What are you saying, Mary Sue? You expect us to share her? Live happily ever after?" Colton couldn't believe what he was hearing. He may have shared most his women with Waylon, and the foursome that had included Boyd and Callie may have felt like the most erotic and natural thing in the world, but…

"Yes."

"Yes?"

"I know you boys are used to sharing women, but Callie's different. I've known you boys since you were in diapers, and you've confided in me more times than I can count. I'm telling you that you can have your happily ever after with Callie, all three of you boys. When you open your eyes, you'll see it, too."

Mary Sue shook her head in exasperation and left the room. Colton had always trusted her advice in the past. She had some sixth sense when it came to relationships and human nature. How could she be right in this case?

"What do you think of that?" asked Waylon.

"A bride for three," muttered Boyd, lost in his own world.

"We need to talk with Callie. All of us. Any final decision is hers. If she chooses one of us, or all of us, I'm eager to hear her opinion," said Colton, rising from his seat.

Chapter Twenty-one

After calling Josh's house from a pay phone to ensure her grandfather was okay, she spent the night in her truck. She awoke the next morning, stiff and sore from the cramped quarters in her truck cab. Callie sat up and squinted against the daylight streaming in through the windshield. Nobody would find her. She'd made sure of that, parking off the road in a remote field that used to be used for grazing. Her mind had been ready to snap the night before, and she couldn't deal with any men or any more lies. With the light of day, she felt rejuvenated mentally and felt better able to refrain from the urge to cry and feel sorry for herself. She had to find out if there was any way to get her farm back from the Blacks and had to find a place for her grandpa to stay if she couldn't.

Paddy. She wouldn't let them keep her horse. They'd probably sell him, along with her other belongings, the first chance they got. She'd have to sneak onto her own property and steal her horse from under their noses. The night before, she had driven by a few times and couldn't believe the amount of people occupying the little farm. Spotlights were set up, and teams of workers spread around like ants. She couldn't believe there had actually been a fortune of oil under her land all along. If only she'd known.

Callie parked her truck a half mile from her house and began walking along the edge of the forest that would bring her behind her house. With her muffler, or lack thereof, she'd announce her arrival if she didn't continue on by foot. Once she snuck on her property and got Paddy, she'd ride him out of there. That's pretty much where her plan ended.

As she neared her property, she could hear heavy equipment and a multitude of men's voices. Through a clearing in the trees, she saw her dogs tied up, barking like rabid animals. Her poor babies, she'd have to let them loose, too. She knew they'd follow her and Paddy obediently. They had already begun excavating her east field. Her grandpa would have a fit if he saw the sight she saw. Their family home had turned into a construction zone in a matter of hours.

Callie crept along the back of her house, trying her best to be stealthy. She just needed a clean line of sight for a few seconds to race across the clearing to the open barn doors. Her heart beat a mile a minute from fear when she should be furious for losing everything.

When her break came, she took it, running as fast as her legs could carry her. Once inside the barn, she breathed a breath of relief and immediately set her search in motion. There they were, their rumps protruding from the last two stalls. She smiled, feeling a sense of peace from the familiar sight of Paddy. Clicking her tongue softly so he'd recognize her, she entered the stall and caressed his muzzle. If only he could talk, because she didn't have a friend in the world.

"Okay, boy. You've gotta be fast, and the terrain is still soft from the rain, so we'll have to be extra careful," she whispered. After untying his lead, she backed him out, flinching as his hooves clomped heavily on the concrete center of the barn. Once free from the confines, Callie decided she should release the other Quarter Horse, too. He'd follow Paddy on the way out like a second skin.

"Stay there, boy." She left Paddy to unsecure the other horse. While in the stall, she heard voices approaching the barn, and her blood froze cold.

"Who let that horse free?"

"No clue, Mr. Smith."

Smith! Her icy blood warmed over and began to heat until she felt like a kettle ready to blow. His voice, the very thought of his deceit and how he took advantage of her, made her livid. She continued to free the second horse, planning to rush out and throw herself up on Paddy bareback before she could be stopped.

"There. Someone's in that stall. Check it out!" said Jack Smith. The other man followed his order, and then more footsteps could be heard entering the barn. She felt like a caged animal with nowhere to run.

"I think it's her. The young blonde you warned us about," said the worker, looking down on her as she crouched in the corner. Already caught, she stood up tall and exited the stall.

"Well, well, well. Look who we have here." Mr. Smith laughed with that superior sound that made her want to throttle him.

"I suppose you're pleased with yourself. The Blacks hired the right man. You'd have to be a heartless bastard to steal from innocent people."

"Honey, just stop. It's done, get over it. Go find that Evans fellow. He's around here somewhere. I've promised him a pretty penny for his help in all this, so he'll be able to buy you a nicer place than this dump. See, I'm not so bad, after all." He winked at her and then left the barn as if she were of no threat or consequence. She stood there idly in the center of the barn, the same place where Waylon and Colton had tied her down and played their dirty games with her. Damn, she was a fool through and through.

"Hey!" she called out. "How did Josh help you?"

"You'll have to ask him. I promised not to rain on his parade."

She didn't have to look far for him. Callie practically bumped into him as she raced out of the barn, pulling Paddy behind her.

"Callie. Where have you been? I've been worried sick." She wanted to believe Josh. Wanted to collapse into his waiting arms and let him help her, but she wouldn't. She had a bad feeling about him and the Smith fiasco.

"Sure. What did you do to help Jack Smith? Did you have a hand in me losing my farm?"

"Of course not! I told you, I tried to help you after those Black brothers tried to steal everything from you."

"Well, apparently they succeeded, so you weren't much help." Callie narrowed her gaze and tried to garner his intentions. "Why would he pay you? You've done something, haven't you?"

"Callie, stop talking foolish. We have to move on and make the best of this." He tried to put an arm around her shoulder, but she shrugged him off.

"You snuck into my place looking for mortgage papers. Why?" Her suspicions rose as she slowly pieced together the mystery around her.

He ran his hands through his blond hair and sighed heavily. "Look, they were gonna get your place one way or another. Trust me, I looked into helping you, but there was no way. When oil's involved, men get bloodthirsty for money. All I did was ensure that I'd get paid so that I could help you in the aftermath. Don't you see? I did it all for you. For us."

"Oh, my God, Josh. What have you done? If you tell me you sold me out to the Blacks, God help you."

"Be reasonable."

Every man on Earth besides her grandpa had screwed her good, from her father to the Blacks to Josh and Mr. Smith. The one man who had been good to her all her life was going to be the ultimate victim in all this because she couldn't take care of him.

"Get away from me. I don't want you or your dirty money."

"Callie. Please."

A truck raced up the driveway, braking abruptly, followed by several door slams. It was the Black brothers, all three of them. They raced toward her as if she needed rescuing. Just seeing their faces after the betrayal was too much. She realized that she really did love them, and the fact that everything she'd thought they felt for her was an act hurt her deeply.

"Thank God we found you, woman! Where have you been?" asked Colton, pulling her into his strong embrace. She tugged away, but he wouldn't have it.

"What do you care? Any of you? You've gotten what you wanted, so stay away from me."

"What is she talking about?" asked Waylon.

"Damned if I know," said Colton.

"Look, just stop the act. Jack Smith and Josh told me everything I needed to know."

Boyd took up ground behind Josh while Waylon guarded him from the front. "What exactly did he tell you, Callie?" asked Boyd.

"That you used me all along to get the oil on my land! I should have known better than to trust three womanizers. I was an idiot to fall in love with any one of you."

"You love us?" asked Colton, ignoring everything else she'd said.

She growled and twisted in his embrace. "Yes, I loved you, all three of you. And for what? You played me for a fool and walked away with a clean conscience."

"Callie, we never took your land," said Boyd. "Whatever's going on here lies with this boy and Mr. Smith, not us. I promised you that I'd never abandon you, Callie, and I meant that."

"That kid doesn't need to hear the rest of this. Get rid of him, Boyd." Colton waited as Boyd dragged Josh to his old truck and slammed him against the side with orders to leave. The yellow-belly didn't waste time in his retreat.

"Taken care of," said Boyd as he returned. The three men huddled around her, making her dizzy. She didn't know what to believe or think at this point. Callie desperately wanted to believe that the Blacks were not at fault for her nightmarish situation and truly cared about her, loved her, even.

"We came here last night to talk to you, but you were already gone," said Colton. "You worried us sick, by the way."

Waylon continued. "We love you, darlin'. All of us. If you'll have us, we want to be a family, all four of us. I know it's not your normal kind of—"

Callie cut him off. "No, it's perfect."

"What?" Colton gripped her shoulders and forced her to make eye contact with him.

"I said that sounds perfect. The fact that I loved all three of you had been eating away at me. No way could I choose between any of you. Hearing that you're all willing to share me couldn't be sweeter to my ears."

Colton swung her up in his arms and twirled her around. "Don't you worry about this mess, darlin'. We'll have it all straightened out in no time. From now on, let us do the worrying."

"Is this real?" she asked in disbelief.

Boyd kissed her cheek. "Oh, it's real. You get three knights in shining armor instead of just one. We never plan on letting you out of our sight again."

Chapter Twenty-two

Three weeks later, Callie and her three cowboys sat around a picnic table behind the Black Corporation, admiring their wedding certificate. Well, she was officially married to Waylon, seeing that they were closest in age. That little factor had been a great debate amongst the men, but she assured them that it didn't matter whose name was on the document because she knew in her heart she belonged to the three of them.

Since Mr. Smith had forged documents obtained by Josh to get her farm, they were able to hire a lawyer to straighten the entire mess out. Smith had found out that the Johnson ranch had oil when he first began the Blacks' restructuring plan and wanted it for himself. The Johnson ranch was in the rightful owners' hands now and always would be. She wouldn't allow her men to charge Josh. He had just been a fool in love. Callie knew he'd find a nice girl to settle down with in time. They decided to stand off on the oil drilling while Callie's grandpa was still alive. Money wasn't as important as the older man's happiness in his final years. Besides, her husbands had more than enough money. They constantly bought her stuff from town—clothes, lingerie, riding gear, and anything she mentioned wanting.

"Now what?" asked Waylon as they passed the paper around.

"Well, a marriage means that a honeymoon's in store, doesn't it?" asked Boyd. Callie glanced around the barley fields around them. The ranchers were given the day off for the wedding, so the area was barren of human life. The thought of sharing her men on their official honeymoon, in addition to not having a worry in the world, made her body heat in anticipation.

"Well, since I'm the oldest, I think I should have dibs," said Colton, gently tilting Callie's chin toward him. He leaned over and kissed her on the lips.

"Well, that's just a terrible idea," said Waylon. "Since I'm the official husband, I should be first."

Boyd shoved Waylon in the shoulder. "We warned you never to rub that in our faces, little brother."

Callie climbed up onto the wooden picnic table, still wearing the simple white dress that she'd worn to the ceremony. Mary Sue, her maid of honor, had driven her grandpa back home. It sure felt right to have him give her away at the wedding. She'd never cried so much in her life. Her eyes were still a bit swollen from the day's events.

"You boys are not going to fight on our wedding day. I only get one chance to play the bride, don't ruin it for me," she scolded.

"You choose, then, sweet thing." Colton kissed her nose.

"I never plan on choosing, not when I don't have to. I'll have all of you today because it's our special day. I'm on the pill now, and I can't wait to feel your cocks riding me bareback."

"Fuck. Me." Colton growled and climbed up on the picnic table, forcing her to her back. He kissed her as he fluffed up the layers of her dress to her waist.

Callie cupped his face, so smooth from being clean shaven for the wedding, and kissed him with all the passion she felt at the moment. They all looked edible in their black suits. Good thing they weren't rentals because she planned to rip the material off their bodies if they didn't get naked soon. She wanted to see and feel their muscled flesh under her hands and against her skin.

As Colton kissed her, she felt the menagerie of hands undressing her, pulling her pantyhose and undies free of her body. She was swarmed with sensation from all directions, not knowing who touched her, kissed her, and squeezed her. It didn't matter. They were all hers, forever. She reveled in the feeling of belonging, of being wanted.

"Colton, control yourself," said Boyd, pulling him back. Callie panted, wanting his weight pressed over her again. "I want to taste our wife before you bury your cock inside her."

"Wait!" Waylon pulled out a long, black blindfold from his breast pocket. "This will be more fun. Darlin', you won't know who's touching you or fucking you." He tied the silky black material around Callie's eyes. She couldn't see a thing, but her blindness heightened all her other senses. It really didn't matter that she wouldn't know who was who because they were all one to her.

Rough hands parted her legs farther, fluffing up the layers of her dress. The summer breeze caressed her exposed flesh as she lay back on the picnic table in the open field behind the barns. When a hot mouth covered her cunt, she couldn't hold back a scream. Whoever continued to suck her clit did so without mercy. The intensity of pleasure was too much for her to handle. She needed a respite, a deep breath, but wasn't granted one.

Callie bucked and twisted, trying to free herself as she squealed like a wild woman. "No more!" she cried.

Her only response was low chuckles of dark pleasure. Numerous hands pinned her down, forcing her to accept the hot mouth invading her most private parts. "She's a feisty one. It'll take us a lifetime to teach her how to behave during sex," said Colton with amusement in his voice.

"Good thing she's ours, then. I look forward to training her," said Waylon.

She couldn't believe it was Boyd between her legs, not allowing her mercy. But as the minutes passed, she broke free from the state of constant overstimulation and entered the world of pre-orgasmic bliss. Her moans carried across the fields as she dropped her legs loosely to the sides, accepting Boyd's ministrations. She tried to arch into his mouth, wanting more because she was so close to climax, but the many hands continued to secure her. Her dress was unzipped and pulled over her head, leaving her naked besides her white heels. When two hungry mouths began to devour her breasts, she erupted, her orgasm bursting outward from her cunt. She clawed her hands in each head over her chest and screamed as her orgasmic contractions rocked her body.

"Good girl, Callie. You're ready for us now." Ready? She had no power left in her to resist. Her body was hot and pliant, and she felt dirty and kinky after her release. When she realized she wanted to be spanked, punished, and forced to perform, she decided to be a bad girl to get their attention.

A hot, thick cock prodded her lips. "Suck my dick, sweet thing. I wanna feel your lips wrapped around me." She denied Colton, giving him a quick lick and turning her head.

"She's not listening, Colt." She knew it was Waylon's hands that gathered her full breasts in his palms, kneading them as he spoke. "Maybe she's not such a good girl."

"What do you think, then? Spanking?"

"Definitely!" agreed Boyd. Hearing her men and not seeing them in their sexy black suits or touching them was too difficult to bear. She pulled the silk from her eyes and peered to the side.

"Ah, ah, ah, darlin'. You're cheatin'." Colton sat up on the table and then stretched her over his lap. His white shirt was mostly undone, revealing the firm muscles of his chest. Her core thrummed with anticipation of her spanking.

Colton rubbed her ass, creating friction and heat over her exposed skin. She clenched, waiting for the first strike. Of course, he didn't spank her until she relaxed, making her squeal. The men laughed, enjoying her punishment too much. Waylon stood beside her. He smiled down at her as he sucked his thumb into his mouth, the sun brightening his blue eyes. He pressed his moistened thumb into her ass, his fingers playing with her clit. She moaned and dropped heavily over Colton's lap, her eyes lolling back in her head.

"Do you want to be fucked?" asked Waylon. She nodded eagerly. "Good, then let's play. Colton, loosen your britches." Callie couldn't see what orchestrated with her head upside down. The men helped her to her feet as Colton sat on the picnic table, smearing lube over his ready cock. Still mostly dressed in his dress pants and white shirt, he looked edible—clean shaven, but still sporting his disheveled, dirty-blond mop of hair.

"Okay, sugar. Colt and Boyd are going to fuck you at the same time. Can you handle both their cocks again, rubbing together inside you at once?"

She licked her lips and nodded.

"Good. Boyd, help me lift her." The two men turned her around and lifted her up under the shoulders with ease. They were big men, and lifting a slight thing like her was nothing to them. "You're gonna sit on Colt's lap. His dick is gonna spear your ass, so try and relax."

Colton held her around the waist from behind, and the other men helped lower her over his rigid cock. She felt every inch embed into her ass, filling her with that unique erotic sensation that she was learning to revel in. But she wanted more. There was nothing like getting double-fucked, being filled to the max with all that steely man-flesh. The men supporting her moved away as Colton took control, holding her securely in his lap, his erection buried to the hilt inside her. Boyd stripped off his shirt and unzipped his pants. She wrapped her arms around his neck as he moved in to kiss her. Feeling his firm, muscled skin, warmed by sunshine, was heavenly. She pulled him closer, kissing him deeper as Colton peppered kisses at the side of her neck.

Boyd reached low, dipping his cock in her juices. She clenched around Colton, making him groan, so eager to be filled. When Boyd thrust up her cunt, wedging in next to Colton's cock, she thought she'd orgasm in that perfect moment.

"Jesus Christ, woman, you're tight," muttered Boyd as he thrust his hips, pushing deep. She loved the feel of riding the men bareback.

Her sensations were magnified, heated, and all consuming. She gripped Boyd's shoulders as the men shared her body, fucking her as a team. Her next release was already building, making her pussy spasm spontaneously.

"You're not allowed to come, Callie. Behave yourself!" warned Waylon, watching the action as he pumped his shaft in his fist.

"Oh, fuck!" shouted Colton as his hot seed filled her ass. She needed to come, wanted to come, but tried to obey Waylon and hold back. Boyd followed next, thrusting hard as heated sprays of ejaculate filled her cunt.

"What about me?" she complained, having been so close and robbed of her orgasm.

"It's my turn, sweetheart. Lay her on the table."

Both semi-flaccid dicks slid out of her as the men gently lowered her to her feet and then hoisted her up onto the table, where their jackets were laid as a makeshift blanket. Callie felt the hot cum seeping out of her body, down her legs, in a sticky mess.

Waylon climbed over her, nudged her legs open with his strong thigh, and impaled her with his cock in one quick thrust. He was wound tight, his dick harder than the wood she lay on. The sex was wet and dirty but so fucking good. Callie held on as Waylon went savage on her body, promising her the orgasm she waited for.

Together, they came, Callie's pussy milking him, claiming him, as her walls contracted around his length. Waylon groaned and stiffened as he released his seed inside her, filling her to the brink. She felt at peace. These three perfect, beautiful cowboys who could have any woman they wanted, wanted her. They'd married her, promised her forever, and brought her to new sexual peaks.

The summer day was warm, the grass around them thick and lush. They lay there together, staring up at the cotton-white clouds lazily drifting by, as they savored the after-sex bliss. Paddy grazed off in the distance with the many black Arabians on the Black ranch.

She nuzzled in the crook of Boyd's arm. "I can't believe that I hated all of your guts only a couple months ago."

"I still remember the day you showed up at the ranch raising hell. You were quite the spitfire," said Boyd.

"Just because we're all married now doesn't mean I'm going to change my ways. I'll always be pushy, mouthy, and demanding. You knew what you were getting into."

Colton rolled toward her and stroked her side with a featherlight touch. "I wouldn't want you any other way. I like my women feisty. But when it comes to intimacy…that's a different story."

Callie couldn't agree more. She loved to let it all go when they had sex. Trying to steal her farm was one form of takeover she wouldn't tolerate, but controlling her mind and body in the bedroom was something she relished.

"Don't worry, I'm prepared for a full-scale cowboy domination."

THE END

www.staceyespino.com

ABOUT THE AUTHOR

Stacey Espino resides in beautiful Ontario, Canada where she is busy raising her five school-aged children. She loves being a Canadian, but could do without the brutal winters. When she's not escaping into the romantic settings she creates on her laptop, she's reading one of the many books threatening to overtake her bedroom. With a passion for the paranormal, she wrote Fearless Desires, the first Siren-Bookstrand novel in her Immortal Love series.

Also by Stacey Espino

Siren Publishing, Inc.
www.SirenPublishing.com

LaVergne, TN USA
18 February 2011
217196LV00004B/235/P